THE RULES OF MARRIAGE

'It does seem unfair that ladies have to be married before they have lovers,' declared the Honourable Charlotte Rivers. Only seventeen, innocent and impetuous, for her life is an immense delight. Her happiness seems complete when her childhood hero, the fascinating Kit Brancaster, declares his love. When a rapturous honey-moon in Italy is followed by the birth of an heir Charlotte imagines that their conubial bliss will go on for ever. Still very young, however, Charlotte is misled by the people around her into accepting Regency society's double standards. She plunges headlong into an affair with disastrous results, from which she emerges with her eyes open, at last. But is it too late?

THE RULES OF MARRIAGE

SHEILA BISHOP

**FIRECREST
BATH**

First published 1979
by
Hurst & Blackett Limited
This Large Print edition published by
Firecrest Publishing Limited
Bath
by arrangement with
Hutchinson Publishing Group Limited
1980

ISBN 0 85119 047 2

© Sheila Bishop 1979

British Library Cataloguing in Publication Data

Bishop, Sheila
    The rules of marriage. – Large print ed.
    I. Title
    823'.9'1F   PR6052.1796/

    ISBN 0–85119–047–2

Photoset, printed and bound
in Great Britain by
REDWOOD BURN LIMITED
Trowbridge & Esher

CHAPTER ONE

On a warm September morning in 1815 Kit Colbrook, who was the third Marquess of Brancaster, walked in the garden at Leavening with Lady Olivia Chance. She had been his mistress for several years; an affair so discreet and long-accepted that no one found anything remarkable in seeing them together—neither Lady Olivia's other guests, nor her servants, and certainly not Mr Chance, that pillar of Lord Liverpool's Ministry, who was in the library dealing with his despatch boxes.

Only the Rivers girls, high above them in the school-room window, watched the sauntering couple with a keen interest.

'Cousin Olivia is lucky!' sighed fifteen-year-old Mary. 'Brancaster is so *very* handsome, isn't he? And much younger than St Eudo.'

'Well, but Cousin Olivia is younger than Mama.' The Honourable Charlotte Rivers was seventeen, just on the point of coming out. 'I must say, it does seem unfair that ladies have to be married before they can have lovers.'

'For heaven's sake, Char!' exclaimed their

elder sister Amelia, 'do mind what you say. Little pitchers.'

They all glanced at their nine-year-old cousin Louisa Chance, the actual owner of the schoolroom, who was sitting on a stool, nursing her black and white kitten. She was much too young to hear about such things. They themselves were not supposed to know that their mother was the mistress of Lord St Eudo, and with everyone else they respected the convention of their own ignorance, though the knowledge was so deeply implanted in their consciousness that they took it for granted. Lady Rivers was a famous beauty. Christened Amelia, she had always been called Aimée—beloved—and that suited her, for she was adored by her husband, her lover, her children and her friends, living in a climate of generous sentiments and tender sensibility.

Her elder daughter had inherited nothing but her name, which no one tried to shorten. Plain and pale she was dreadfully shy. She should have been downstairs with the grown-up house-party, instead of hiding in the schoolroom. Mary was a jolly pudding of a girl whose looks would not improve for a year or two.

Charlotte had just realized with astonishment that she was getting rather pretty. It

2

was a source of secret triumph mixed with apprehension. She stared down at the foreshortened view of her idol Lord Brancaster, and wished she was a dashing widow of twenty-five.

Louisa came up to join them at the open window.

'What are you looking at?'

'At Lord Brancaster's dog,' said Charlotte promptly. 'Do you see him on the grass?'

Louisa craned forward, and the kitten slipped through her arms like quicksilver and popped out of the window.

Louisa gave a wail of dismay. 'Poor Tibs, he'll be killed!'

Her cousins assured her that Tibs would be safe, he would know by instinct how to climb and soon come in again. But though they called him, Tibs did not come and presently they heard faint, plaintive cries of distress. He had obviously climbed too enthusiastically and was afraid to come down. Louisa became distracted, and Charlotte offered to get out on the roof and look for him.

Her sisters exclaimed in horror. 'Char, you mustn't! It's too dangerous.'

'Oh, fudge!' said Charlotte. 'No one could possibly fall off the roof of the orangery.'

She pushed up the sash window to its full extent and stepped out.

The orangery, built on to the side of the Palladian mansion, was only two storeys high and the flat area just below the third-floor window of the house was indeed perfectly safe, being protected at the edge by a balustrade with classical urns. Charlotte could not see the kitten at first, but she could hear pathetic mews, so she followed them until she came to the end of the orangery and then saw the little harlequin creature crouched on a ridge of the tiled roof a few feet away from her.

She called to him but he was afraid to move. She looked about her. The slope of the roof was very gradual just here. By standing on a third-floor window-sill and using a convenient gutter to lever herself upwards, she thought she could get near enough to reach him. She managed this in a sprawling,unladylike scramble, seated herself on the ridge with her feet dangling over the far side, and held out her hand to the kitten.

'Come along, Tibs,' she said coaxingly. 'Aren't you glad to see me?'

Tibs was so glad that he dug all his claws into her wrist and hung his whole weight on them. The pain was excruciating. Startled, Charlotte lost her balance, and they slid slowly down the inner slope of the tiles into a gully about eight feet below.

4

'You silly little fool, Tibs,' said Charlotte, in exactly the voice, exasperated yet calm, which her father had used when she fell off her pony as a child. She had not been frightened, or only for a second, because anyone could see that the gully, with a further peak of tiles rising beyond it, was completely enclosed by the balustrade at one end and a massive chimney-stack at the other. In fact she was now trapped in this enclosure and she did not think she could get out unaided, certainly not while carrying the idiotic kitten who was purring in her arms in the most affectionate way. She could not bring herself to abandon poor Tibs; they would simply have to wait until someone rescued them both.

Her sisters would have given the alarm when she failed to reappear. And what a fuss there would be! Mama's nerves would be affected and everyone else would be cross and say that a girl of seventeen had no business to behave like a hoyden. Charlotte had spent a large part of her childhood wishing she was a boy; she wished for this no longer. She wanted something to be different but she was not sure what.

She settled down to wait, leaning back on one tiled slope with her feet propped against the other. She was tall and slender, her face

5

had just missed her mother's perfect oval.
She knew this but did not realize how much
character was added by her own high cheek-
bones and pointed chin. Her colouring had
an English subtlety: hazel-green eyes and
very fine light-brown hair with changing
lights in it. She wore a round-necked
gingham dress that had become extremely
creased and dirty, and the little cat slept comfortably on her lap in the sun.

Much sooner than she expected, she heard
a man's voice, up on the same level and quite
close.

'Charlotte—where are you?'

'Over here!' she called, wondering who it
was, not her father, she could tell.

The immensely tall figure of a man rose on
to the chimney-stack, his shadow swooped
across the gully. It was Lord Brancaster.

'No bones broken?' he enquired.

'No, none.'

'I'll just go and tell them.'

He vanished and she could hear him
shouting to someone below. Then he came
back.

'They are going to open a skylight further
along to let you in. We may as well stay here
for the present, it's a little more spacious.' He
jumped down to join her. 'So this is the
culprit; he seems to have recovered from his

6

adventure.'

Not a word of censure because she had been so rash, not even a patronizing joke. She had always admired him, from the distance of a child observing her parents' friends. He was six feet four inches tall with shoulders in proportion, but agile and fast-moving. He had a very strong face with a high-bridged nose and firm mouth; his skin had the clear, brown glow of a man who was out of doors a great deal and his raven-black hair curled smoothly across his forehead. His eyes were an unusually brilliant grey, made more intense by the darkness of his eyelashes, which were as long and beautiful as a girl's.

'It was very kind of you to come and look for me,' said Charlotte, slightly overawed. 'I suppose my sisters called for help? Does my mother know? Is she very much alarmed?'

'Not unreasonably,' said Brancaster. 'The person who is kicking up the greatest commotion is Louisa, and I am sorry to say she is thinking only of her cat. Your father could not be found immediately, so I volunteered to make sure you were safe. But how did you get into this crevasse?'

He listened to her adventure, leaning across to stroke Tibs, who flicked an ear and purred vigorously in his sleep.

'An engaging little fellow, though I'm

7

sorry he scratched you.'

'He didn't mean to. Do you like cats, Lord Brancaster? Most men don't.'

'Cats are sensible beasts. Look how well they get on with horses.' He told her that his favourite hunter had a ginger tom who always slept in his manger.

It was odd to be alone with him in this curious place which felt like the inside of a boat. After a slight pause, he spoke again, in a different voice.

'Why don't I see something of you downstairs? Oh yes, I know you're not out yet, but why aren't you? You must be eighteen?'

'Seventeen. I'm coming out in February, when everyone goes back to London after the Recess.'

Parliament sat from February to July. Social life flourished during those months, when so many people of consequence found it necessary to be in London. The Marquess of Brancaster and Charlotte's father Lord Rivers were both members of the House of Lords.

'And then you enter the lists at Almack's?'

Charlotte made a face.

'What's the matter with Almack's?' he enquired.

'Oh well—nothing, I suppose. Everybody goes there and it would be dreadful not to get

8

tickets. Only they call it the marriage-market and I hate the idea of being put on show. And besides, it sounds so stuffy. You have to be approved by the patronesses, and they think it is improper for young girls to waltz.'

'Do you know how to waltz?'

'Not yet,' admitted Charlotte, 'but I am determined to learn.'

'I should enjoy teaching you. What a pity this gully isn't a little wider, we could begin at once.'

Charlotte looked straight at him and asked, 'Are you trying to flirt with me, Lord Brancaster?'

The grey eyes were amused. 'Do you know, Charlotte, I believe I was!'

Another silence, during which Charlotte could hear her heart thumping and hoped he could not hear it too.

Then he asked abruptly, 'How much longer do you remain at Leavening?'

'Only until Wednesday. Then we are going home to Surrey while my mother and father are at Brighton. At least that was the plan, but I think we are all to spend a few days in the London house, so that Amelia can go to the dentist. She has been having toothache.'

'I pity her.'

'Yes, and it is a front tooth, so if it has to come out Mama says she must have riveted

9

into the gap. And what do you think these imitation teeth are made of? The tusk of a rhinoceros! Did you ever hear of anything so barbarous?'

'It is quite shocking,' agreed Brancaster with a perfectly serious face.

Charlotte was checked by a sudden misgiving. 'I ought not to have told you that about Amelia. You won't repeat it, will you, my lord? It would make her an object of ridicule.'

'I won't say a word to embarrass Amelia. Only think how the patronesses of Almack's would feel if they found they had let in a young lady wearing the horn of a rhinoceros!'

Charlotte laughed so much that she was taken by surprise when a footman with a short step-ladder arrived at the chimney-stack to announce that the trapdoor was now open. She and Tibs were conducted safely back into the house.

Louisa was waiting for them on the top landing and hugged them both indiscriminately, before carrying Tibs off to be revived with a saucer of warm milk. She was delighted with Charlotte's performance, which no one else was.

Lady Rivers, downstairs in the drawing-room, murmured, 'I do wish you would not be so dreadfully rash, dearest. I know you are very brave, but I am not, and I have been in a perfect fidget.'

'I'm sorry, Mama. I didn't think.'

Lady Rivers was fashionably dressed in a straight, narrow gown with a high-waisted spencer, and seemed far too young to be the mother of her three daughters, yet she still somehow conveyed the flowing, romantic softness of her own youth, when girls had worn tumbling ringlets and large hats like sailing-ships. She sat looking fragile and exquisite between her husband and her lover, one fanning her with a copy of the *Morning Post* and the other solicitously holding her vinaigrette.

'It is about time you started thinking, Char,' said Lord Rivers, laying down the newspaper. He was a thin, active man in his late forties, his hair just beginning to turn grey. Charlotte was his favourite child; she was nearly faultless in his eyes, except when she did anything to upset her mother.

Lord St Eudo said nothing and looked as he usually did: suave, languid and faintly amused.

Her cousin and hostess Lady Olivia Chance eyed Charlotte with disfavour and said she would have to change her dress. She was a handsome, capable woman, and if she had found it necessary to rescue a cat from a

11

roof she would have managed without getting so dirty.

Lord and Lady Rivers expressed their gratitude to Brancaster.

'It was extremely kind of you to take so much trouble. Charlotte, have you thanked Lord Brancaster properly?'

'Yes, Mama,' said Charlotte, struggling to hide her mortification at being treated like a child. 'Thank you again, my lord.'

'It was a pleasure, Miss Charlotte,' said Brancaster, smiling directly into her eyes.

She was truly grateful to him for that prefix, indicating that he at least considered her a young lady not a little girl. He emphasized this by courteously opening the door for her as she left the room.

CHAPTER TWO

Charlotte did not see Brancaster to speak to again before the Rivers family left Wiltshire for London, where the unlucky Amelia was taken to two different dentists who could not agree upon the right treatment. By this time, needless to say, her toothache had stopped. Charlotte and Mary passed the time looking at the fashions in old copies of the *Ladies' Monthly Magazine* and going for walks with their governess Miss Plummer.

On Tuesday, coming home to Berkeley Street in time for luncheon, they were informed by the butler that her ladyship wished to see Miss Charlotte immediately.

Charlotte went to her mother's dressing-room where she found both her parents waiting for her. They looked odd in some way, unnaturally stiff, she so carefully arranged on the sofa and he standing just behind, the light from the window falling on his thin, kind face and greying hair. They might have been posing to have their portraits painted.

'Sit down, my love,' said Lady Rivers. 'Papa and I have something very particular to discuss with you. Tell me, that day at Leavening when you were on the roof, did Lord Brancaster say anything to you?'

Charlotte stared. 'Well, of course he did, Mama! We talked a great deal. He was very amusing.'

What was all this about? Even as she replied she began to feel uncomfortable, remembering a few of the amusing things she had said herself. Perhaps he had found her forward and pert? He had given no sign at the time, but suppose he had commented to Cousin Olivia—after all, he was in love with her. And suppose Cousin Olivia had written to Mama warning her that Charlotte did not know how to behave in a grown-up conversation with a gentleman. The idea was too mortifying to bear.

'You are blushing, so I think you must guess what I mean,' said Lady Rivers. 'Brancaster came this morning to call on Papa—'

'Is he in London? I thought he was still at Leavening.'

'He drove up on purpose,' said Lord Rivers. 'To ask for my permission, Char, he wants to make you an offer.'

Charlotte was so astounded that she was really unable to speak, a very unusual condition with her.

'Of course it is ridiculous,' said her father. 'You aren't even out. If it had been anyone

14

else, I should have sent him packing. But I thought you ought to have the chance to speak for yourself. And besides—'

He broke off, perhaps he thought it indelicate to say she would never get a better offer.

Charlotte had recovered her tongue. 'Why should he want to marry me?'

They hastened to tell her. He thought she was very pretty and lively—yes, he had said some charming things about her which would make her quite vain. And a man of thirty-one, with his responsibilities, wanted to choose a suitable wife and settle down. . . .

Charlotte knew all this; what she could not make out was why Brancaster had selected her out of so many possible aspirants. While her parents talked, a different train of thought was running through her mind. Was it something to do with Cousin Olivia? Of course a man like Brancaster would want to marry so that he could have an heir, but he might still want to continue his affair with Olivia, and perhaps they thought this would be easier if he chose a very young and inexperienced wife who was a member of the same family. She was not going to marry him on those terms. Only how was she to know? Could she bring herself to ask her parents? No, it was impossible; they would be so shocked to find she was not quite as innocent

15

as they supposed. The enigmatic presence of Lord St Eudo seemed to hover in the room.

Abruptly she asked, 'Can I see Lord Brancaster alone?'

Her mother was taken aback. 'Certainly you will have to give him your answer—but my dearest Charlotte, you cannot have made up your mind so soon? It is a very serious step—'

'No, I didn't mean that, Mama. Can I meet him before I make up my mind?'

Her parents exchanged glances.

'Well, I don't see the harm,' said Lord Rivers. 'How else is she to decide whether she likes him well enough?'

This momentous meeting took place next day in the back drawing-room at Berkeley Street. Lord Brancaster was already there when her mother sent Charlotte in to join him. He stood up and held out his hand.

'My dear Charlotte—how do you do?'

Their fingers just touched. He was looking dauntingly handsome in a swallow-tail coat, snowy cravat and skin-tight pantaloons. She had been obliged to put on her new autumn dress of dark blue merino, a ridiculously childish garment in which to receive a suitor; her mother's maid had tried to dress her hair more fashionably, which had not appeased Charlotte much, for she now felt she was

16

neither flesh, fowl nor good red herring. She was also wearing a furious scowl, though she was not aware of this.

'Come and sit down,' said Brancaster. 'We have plenty to talk about, haven't we? We are both a little nervous, I expect.'

She did not think he was in the least nervous.

'I hope I haven't offended you,' he added, smiling at her.

'No, of course not! You have paid me a very great compliment, sir.'

'I thought you might be annoyed at my having gone straight to your father, instead of trying to fix my interest with you first. Some girls would feel that a very poor-spirited way for a lover to behave, and I promise you I would not have done so, only I couldn't think how we were to meet. I really could not pay my addresses under the nose of your governess. It would not be at all the thing.'

He said this in such a comical way that she could not help laughing.

'There, that's better,' he said.

But it wasn't better, it was worse. Every moment she spent with him she was more fascinated, more convinced that he was exactly the man who would suit her, but if he had simply proposed because she would not disturb the even course of his affair with

Cousin Olivia, then she must refuse him. Better marry without love at all than for a love that was so one-sided.

'What's the matter, Char? Can't you tell me?' he asked gently.

It was infernally difficult. She had not realized how awkward this was going to be. She stared down at the pattern on the carpet, at her shoes, at his polished hessians, clenched and unclenched her fingers on the arm of the chair. Only the mental image of herself as a fidgeting, tongue-tied schoolgirl forced her to look at him and say in a clear, steady voice, 'May I ask you, Lord Brancaster, whether you want to marry me because it would be the most convenient arrangement for my Cousin Olivia?'

'Who the devil gave you that idea?'

The grey eyes actually seemed to flash for a second.

'No one.' She was almost quelled by the note she heard in his voice, but she persisted. 'No one has ever told me—that's why there is no one else I can ask. Mama thinks, you see, that we don't understand about—about the friends ladies have after they are married. Only, of course, one hears things, and a good many of the other girls we know have mothers and aunts who—I don't want you to think that I am being missish or prim or that

18

I am criticizing Cousin Olivia. But I should not care to be in a sort of rivalry with her, for I should be bound to lose,' concluded Charlotte frankly.

Brancaster had listened to this in growing discomfort. He got up and began to walk about the room.

'I had no idea—it never dawned on me that you might be aware—I've no sisters of my own. My dearest girl, there is no question of your having any rivals, and certainly not Olivia. I swear to you, that is all over. And if I had found it necessary to marry while I had a connection with another woman, I certainly shouldn't have chosen a member of the same family.'

'Wouldn't you?' she asked, interested.

He came to rest in front of her, flushed and uncertain. 'Do you mind very much, Charlotte? Knowing this story, has it completely sunk me in your esteem?'

'Oh no,' said Charlotte earnestly.

As a matter of fact it had made him even more attractive, though she did not like to say so.

'I don't think I could bear it if you hated me,' he said. 'I fell in love with you, quite suddenly, last week. One can hardly call it love at first sight, because I have been seeing you on and off, ever since you were a child.

Only that day on the roof it was different. I looked at you and I knew, that is the girl I want to spend the rest of my life with.'

Charlotte gazed up at him in a state of bliss and wonder.

'I am a good deal older than you, but that is no bad thing, and if you can learn to fall in love with me—'

'I have been in love with you since I was eleven,' said Charlotte simply.

'Good God!'

'Well, I know it sounds silly, and of course I never expected anything to come of it. You were so far beyond my reach, and it takes such a long time to grow up. I thought it would always remain a dream. But now . . .'

'But now . . .' repeated Brancaster, taking her in his arms.

Her mother, coming in a few minutes later, was disconcerted to find her young daughter being quite so passionately embraced by the man she herself had always thought of as belonging to her own sophisticated world.

'Mama, we are engaged,' said Charlotte ecstatically.

Kit Brancaster met Lady Rivers' eye. 'Just as well, don't you think, ma'am?'

Charlotte was radiant. Why, she is really

beautiful thought her mother, a good deal
surprised.

CHAPTER THREE

The wedding took place in November, a simple ceremony in the drawing-room at Berkeley Street, with no one present outside the two families—none of the vulgar public parade that was becoming popular in less aristocratic circles.

Kit's most notable relation was his grandmother, the Dowager Lady Brancaster, an eccentric old High Tory in her late seventies who could remember the Young Pretender dining at her father's house on his way to Derby.

She insisted on coming into the room where Charlotte was being dressed and inspecting the result. Reaching out a bony finger to give her a sharp dig in the midriff, she said, 'You ain't wearing stays!'

'No, ma'am.' Charlotte gazed candidly back at the old image in her rouge and wig. 'Do you think Lord Brancaster will mind?'

This amused the Dowager. 'Mind? Not he! But you be careful, miss—loose dressing leads to loose morals. More woman have kept their virtue because they couldn't lie down with their stays on than for any other reason.'

'She really is outrageous!' exclaimed Lady

Rivers, when the old woman had been tactfully evicted. 'You must not mind her coarse way of speaking, my love.'

'I don't, Mama. I like her. And Kit loves her dearly, she took his mother's place.'

Kit's mother had died when he was a baby and it was some years before his father remarried. He had three half-brothers, to whom he was extremely attached; the eldest, Lord Edward Colbrook, was nine years younger than himself. A charming young idler who fancied himself as a dandy, he was attending the wedding, and so was the next brother, Lord Oswald, a histrionic character who had been rusticated from Oxford for writing a pamphlet about tyranny. Lord Hector was at Eton and had not been invited, to his great annoyance.

There were a number of other relations on both sides, and the room was quite crowded when Charlotte sailed in on her father's arm. Her dress was exactly right for a very young bride, for though it was made of priceless Brussels lace, it was perfectly simple, worn over a satin slip and without any trimming. Of all the jewels Kit had given her, today she wore only a gold cross and chain. She was a vision of virginal innocence, yet her face was vivid with confidence and ardour as she moved up the room towards the improvised

23

altar to meet her bridegroom.

Directly after the wedding breakfast Lord and Lady Brancaster set out on the first stage of their continental honeymoon. Charlotte had never been abroad, and although Kit had visited France in 1814, the long war had prevented his making the Grand Tour, so they were able to discover Florence, Venice and Rome together as a background to the happy private world in which they were discovering each other. By the late spring of 1815 they had travelled as far south as Naples. Kit rented a villa out beyond Portici; he wanted to study the excavations.

It was May: the sky above Pompeii was a deep and brilliant blue, and surrounding hills a soft and dusky grape colour. Vesuvius looked romote and peaceful, though there was a lazily insolent tuft of smoke floating above it. The lost city had been buried for seventeen centuries under a blanket of petrified ash which had come in time to look like ordinary ground, so the part that was uncovered resembled the open depth of a quarry. But instead of a quarry full of rough stone, the chipping away of volcanic deposit revealed miraculous walls and doors and sculptured surfaces, beautiful statues and the pathetic bones of the people who had made them.

They paused to watch some workmen digging. One of them picked something up and dusted it, while speaking to their guide, who interpreted to Kit.

'If the *bellissima Marchesa* would care for a memento, matters could be arranged . . .'

'Oh, I should like it above all things!' exclaimed Charlotte.

The object was a small alabaster cup encircled by tiny cupids, and she received it from the Neapolitan workman who might himself have been a bronze god.

'Can you believe it has been lying there all these centuries?' she remarked, admiring the milky translucence.

'No,' said Kit coolly, 'I expect it was put there about ten minutes ago.'

'Is it a fake?' she asked, very disappointed.

'It's perfectly genuine.' He took it from her and scrutinized it carefully. 'But these fellows hide some of their smaller finds, so that they can dig them up again at a suitable moment and sell them to any passing milords. It's all shockingly illegal—everything here belongs to the King of Naples.'

He then paid the man for the cup, with only a mild attempt at bargaining to show he was not as stupid as some of the other milords.

Charlotte did not mind knowing that her

knew treasure had come from a different part of the ruins; because she could now associate it with any of the touching stories they were told, of faithful dogs beside their masters or mothers protecting their children. Pompeii was a sad place, only it was impossible to feel sad, walking beside Kit along one of the ghostly streets in the pure golden light and feeling almost drunk with beauty and happiness.

Another visitor, an Englishman, was coming towards them. He stopped and called out: 'Kit! Kit Brancaster!'

'Good heavens—Gerard!'

They hurried to meet, laughing and exclaiming.

'My dear fellow—what are you doing here?'

'I came out last week.'

'Well, I am delighted to see you—but you have not met my wife. Charlotte, this is Mr Winton, one of our nearest neighbours at Hartwood.'

He was a fair slight man with a great air of elegance, and she faced the curious, critical glance of someone who wanted to be sure that Kit's impulsive marriage to a schoolgirl had not been a complete disaster.

Kit wanted to know where he was staying. At some wretched inn? But that was ridiculous: he must join them at their villa.

'What, and play gooseberry on your wedding tour? Lady Brancaster would think me uncommonly thick-skinned!'

'No, do come, Mr Winton,' said Charlotte quickly. 'We have been married six months, and we'll guarantee not to be too honeymoon-ish.'

She caught a gleam of dawning admiration and felt Kit's approval.

So three hours later Gerard Winton was dining with them at the Villa Antonia—or rather, outside the villa, for the meal was set on a marble table under a trellis of vine-leaves. At first the talk was mostly about their travels.

'And may I ask why you are not at West-minster?' Kit presently enquired in mock severity.

'Well, you may ask, my lord, and I shall hardly know how to reply. If I'd had my wits about me, I should have kept out of your way.'

Seeing Charlotte's puzzled expression, Kit said, 'Gerard is the Member for Troughton. That means, you know, he is supposed to be saying in the House of Commons all the things I am too idle to say in the Lords.'

Troughton was a small market town in Essex, two miles from Hartwood Hall, the seat of the Marquess of Brancaster. Only about twenty of the inhabitants had a vote and they were all adherents of dependents of the Colbrook family. It was, in fact, Kit's pocket borough, what some people were now calling a rotten borough.

'I dare say your husband will throw me out at the next election,' said Gerard. And then, turning more seriously to Kit, 'You will soon be wanting the seat for one of your brothers.'

'Which one? Edward is too feather-brained and as for Oswald, we mustn't let him anywhere near the Palace of Westminster or he will probably blow it up. And Hector is barely fifteen. You are safe for a year or two yet.'

Charlotte thought Mr Winton was rather relieved.

The men went on talking about life in London, about people and events she knew nothing of, less even than the fledgling Miss Charlotte she might have been by this time, attending the weekly balls at Almack's Rooms. The moon had risen in a velvet sky, and there was a soft apricot flush on the horizon thrown upwards by the fires bubbling in the crater of Vesuvius. A nightingale was singing in the nearest olive grove.

Charlotte wanted to go to bed, and to insist that Kit came too, so that they could begin making love without any further waste of time. She also wanted to behave like a proper marchioness and to impress his clever, worldly friend. In the end she got up quietly and said good night.

'I am a little sleepy. No, please don't move, Mr Winton. You and Kit have so much to talk over.'

Virtue was rewarded, for Kit joined her in a quarter of an hour and repeated all the delightful and complimentary things Gerard Winton had said about her.

Gerard spent nearly a week at the Villa Antonia and every morning they drove over to the ruins. It was getting very hot. Charlotte had known for some days that she was pregnant, though she had not told Kit, for the rather ridiculous reason that she wanted to climb Vesuvius. A member of the British Ambassador's staff had promised to take them up, and if Kit started worrying about her health, she was afraid he might make her stay behind.

Gerard left them to join some friends who were going to Sicily, and two days later the Vesuvius expedition was finally arranged. They had to start very early and Charlotte felt too sick to eat any breakfast. Luckily Kit was busy arming himself with maps and charts and measuring instruments, so he did not notice. The nausea soon passed off and she was feeling quite well during the first part of the journey, but when they had to leave their open carriage and go on by mule she was alarmingly weak from hunger. The sun was high and seemed to be shining straight down on her head through the flimsy protection of a large straw hat. Her body was soaked with sweat and her muslin dress stuck to her like an eighth skin. The mountain path winding ahead of them was very long and steep; somehow the prospect of plodding through a lava field on the edge of an enormous, red-hot furnace was no longer so attractive.

I won't give in, she thought, gritting her teeth. I won't complain and spoil everything. And then there was a roaring in her ears, reality shrank away into blackness, and the next thing she knew, she was lying on the ground, with Kit kneeling beside her, and Mr Campbell from the Embassy wondering if she had any smelling-salts.

Charlotte did not ask any of the classic questions of swooning females. She knew quite well where she was and why.

'I've never fainted before,' she said, struggling to sit up. 'How silly of me.'

'You were overcome by the heat, my love. It's my fault, I should have told you to bring a parasol. We'll have to turn back, Campbell, as soon as my wife is fit to be moved.'

'Of course, my lord. I'll get the men to rig up a litter.'

Charlotte said she would be perfectly able to sit on her mule, and she did so, with Kit walking beside her and his arm round the back of her saddle to support her if necessary, all the way down to their carriage. Mr Campbell and the mulesters offered to take turns with him, but he was determined to guard over Charlotte himself.

They returned to the villa; she was put to bed in the dark with the shutters closed and immediately fell asleep. When she woke she ate some bread and butter, drank several cups of tea and felt very well indeed. She put on a dress of sea-blue gauze for the evening and went in search of Kit. He was at the marble table, reading. He stood up and took her hand.

'How do you feel now, my love? Come and sit in the shade. Does your head ache?'

'No, not at all. I am completely recovered, thank you.'

'Well, I hope you may be, but I wonder whether I ought to have sent for a doctor. These attacks can be serious.'

'There is nothing wrong with me. In fact, very much to contrary: I am going to have a child.'

She tried to say this with a nonchalant air, like an old married woman who had made the announcement half a dozen times before, though she was watching him closely for the first sign of pride and pleasure.

He was pleased but cautious.

'If that's the answer, it would be splendid news. We had better not count on it, however. A single fainting-fit on a hot day—'

'But I knew already. I've known for nearly a fortnight.'

He said slowly, 'You kept this from me deliberately.'

It was an accusation.

'Yes, but only because—Kit, what's the matter?'

'You stupid little fool!' His voice made her jump. 'To set out on such an expedition, knowing the risk—'

'There was no particular risk that I can see—'

'Of course there was a risk! A pregnant woman cavorting about in the crater of Vesuvius, exposed to violent heat and vertigo and poisonous fumes! Are you so spoilt that you cannot sacrifice a single pleasure, no matter what the consequences may be?'

He was in a freezing temper. The shadow of the vine-leaves fell in a jagged line across his cheek and his eyes were a steely grey. She

32

was astonished and a little frightened that he could be so angry but she was not prepared to show it.

'I think you are making a ridiculous fuss.'

'Do you? Well then, let me tell you, Charlotte, that I won't have you endangering your own health or the survival of my son—'

'I dare say it is a daughter,' she murmured, to provoke him.

'Does a dead child matter less to you if it is a girl?'

Charlotte caught her breath. 'That is a cruel thing to say!'

She swung away from the table and ran off along one of the little paths that criss-crossed the overgrown garden. She heard him calling her name, coming after her, and hurried on. She had to be alone to release this burning pain that was tightening in her heart and throat. How could he be so unkind? Here she was, carrying his child, gladly accepting the discomforts and the ordeal ahead, only to be treated in this heartless way. Not looking where she was going, she caught her foot in a trailing vine and nearly fell headlong down a flight of broken steps. As she flew forwards the dreadful thought flashed through her brain: now I really shall lose our baby. Mercifully, she was able to catch at the balustrade and save herself, but the shock brought her to her senses.

This was no time for tantrums, she had new responsibilities. Perhaps she had been childish and silly, and Kit had the right to tell her so. There was a step on the path and she saw him coming towards her. Their eyes met and they ran into each other's arms.

There was no need for words. They clung together in a deep and silent understanding, their senses half-drowned in love and the scent of oleanders. They stood there so long that a lizard, which Charlotte had scared into a crevice, came out again and played around their feet.

It was the end of their first quarrel.

CHAPTER FOUR

Once he knew about the baby, Kit decided they should return to England. (He found time, before they left, to explore the crater of Vesuvius with Mr Campbell. Charlotte stayed meekly behind at the villa.)

They spent the rest of the year at Kit's family home in Essex. Hartwood Hall was an early Tudor mansion of rose-red brick with additions by Inigo Jones, standing at a place where the countryside changed dramatically. It was like a house on a cliff, poised between two elements. To the south rolled the great forest that divided London from East Anglia. The ground was unusually hilly for Essex, and from the forest's edge it was possible to see for a long way, over and around and between the thick groves of trees. You could make out the dome of St Paul's twenty miles off, on a clear day. To the north, the flat ploughed fields spread wide open to the sun and wind. They were seamed by little woods, hedges and big open ditches. This was good corn-growing country and two windmills stood out on the skyline, both on Colbrook land.

Although they invited relations to stay, as

well as receiving and returning the formal calls of the local gentry, Kit and Charlotte spent the autumn very quietly, making her pregnancy the excuse. It was true that she did feel uncommonly lazy and needed a great deal of sleep. She was happy to be in the country with Kit, continuing the dreamlike isolation of their wedding tour. They planned improvements, shifted furniture and pictures around to see how they looked in different places. Kit told Charlotte some fascinating stories about the famous old house where successive Earls of Brancaster had entertained every English sovereign from Elizabeth to James II.

'But none after that until the present King. We have never cared for usurpers,' he said loftily.

His grandfather, the first Marquess, had found it possible to be a loyal subject of George III, that good Englishman, and the Colbrooks had remained Tory, though so many of their friends among the aristocracy were Whigs.

In January 1817 they came up to London, so that Kit could go to the house of Lords and Charlotte would be near her doctor. She was to be attended by Sir Richard Croft, the celebrated *acoucheur*.

Unlike Charlotte's parents, whose town

house was one of many in a fashionable street, Kit had inherited a mansion which his family had built on their own land just north of the Oxford Road. When the land was developed they had followed the usual custom of giving to the new terraces names with old associations. Brancaster House occupied one entire side of Hartwood Square, at the top of Colbrook Place.

Kit had his three half-brothers living with him. Their Scottish mother had married a highland chief as her second husband and seldom came to London. On the morning of the 22nd January they were all at the breakfast table, even Lord Hector who should have been back at Eton; he had most conveniently broken his wrist in the hunting-field at the end of the holidays.

'I shall go out this morning and watch the fun,' he announced cheerfully. 'Will you come with me, Edward?'

Lord Edward shuddered. He was the only person at the table not enjoying his breakfast. His handsome face as pale as marble, he sat gloomily drinking black coffee.

Kit glanced at him with sympathetic amusement.

'It's always a mistake to drink the punch when you don't know what's in it. Like playing cards with strangers.'

The prodigal winced slightly, and Charlotte wondered if he had been doing that too.

Hector turned to their remaining brother. 'Will you come with me, Oz?'

'I have no desire to see a pack of corrupt old diehards and placemen fooling about in fancy-dress,' said Lord Oswald grandly.

'So let that be a lesson to us,' murmured Kit.

'I'm sorry—I didn't mean you—it's the idea of the Regent going to open that farcical parliament which represents nobody—'

Oswald became hopelessly entangled in his explanation. He had a thin, clever face, like all the Colbrooks but instead of smooth dark hair, his grew in fair wiry curls that sprung up in a bush over his head. Like many earnest people, he was often a little comic. Hector could not resist teasing him.

'What an old Jacobin you are, Oz!'

'Hold your tongue, you puppy!'

Oswald took a sideways swipe at his young brother, knocking over a cream jug. A river of pale, thick cream flowed across the table-cloth between islands of flowery china, butter tubs and toast-racks, hot rolls and spiced buns, honey, Scotch marmalade and all the paraphernalia for making coffee and tea.

'For heaven's sake, Oz!' exclaimed Kit. 'Must you be such an oaf? This isn't a bachelor establishment now, you know, and there is no excuse for turning Charlotte's breakfast-room into a pigsty. As for you, Hector: if you can be so confoundedly witty at this hour of the day you had better go back to school at once.'

He rang the bell for a footman to clear up the disaster.

Hector immediately began to look pathetic, making a great play with his sling. Oswald apologized to Charlotte. He was uneasy in female company and had found it harder to get used to her presence than the other two boys. She did her best to soothe him, she was not at all upset. Having no brothers of her own, she thoroughly enjoyed the masculine society that surrounded her, here and at Hartwood, it was a delightful novelty.

Kit stood up, revealing under his ordinary cutaway coat the knee breeches and white silk stockings of full dress.

'I must go and equip myself for this famous masquerade. Come and help me, Char.'

As they went upstairs together, Charlotte said, 'I do wish I could attend the State Opening. It's all very well for you to laugh, I know I look enormous—like a whale in a pillow-case—but I should be quite respectable under all that red velvet, I'm sure no one would notice.'

'They'd notice if you gave birth on the steps of the throne, my love.'

The baby was due in just over a week.

In his dressing-room Kit's servant was waiting to envelop him in his marquess's robes. The crimson velvet hung heavily from his broad shoulders, black-tipped tails of ermine swirled in snowy softness round the border.

'I must say, I do look very ridiculous,' he remarked, frowning at himself in the cheval-glass.

He kissed Charlotte goodbye, picked up his coronet, and set out for Westminster in the family state coach. She thought privately that he looked magnificent, like a prince in a romance. (Much more like a prince than that fat old man whom everyone despised.)

Edward had gone back to his room, Oswald and Hector went out together, happily arguing. The house was full of servants in the basement, while the nurse and midwife were already installed on the second floor. Charlotte, left to herself, was glad a little later to hear the voices of callers in the hall, and the butler ushered in her sisters Amelia and Mary, accompanied by their former governess Miss Plummer.

'How are you dear Char?' asked Amelia.

40

'Mama thought you might be feeling a little low, so we have come to cheer you up.'

'Oh, this is famous! Do sit down, all of you, and we will be quite cosy.'

It was pleasant sitting round the fire, exchanging family news, looking forward hopefully to Charlotte's baby and Mary's coming-out ball. A light luncheon was brought in, and none of the girls thought much about what might be happening to their parents and Charlotte's husband at the House of Lords.

Until the door was thrown open and Hector appeared, flushed and breathless.

'What do you think? The Regent has been assassinated!'

They gaped at him in horror and wonder. 'It's not possible! How do you know?'

'We were there. Well, not there precisely, because the crowds were so great—you tell them, Oz.'

'We were at the top of Whitehall,' said Oswald. 'We had heard that the delegates from the Hampden Clubs were marching to the House of Commons, to present their petition for universal suffrage. Only we got caught up in such a throng of people and presently there was a terrible outcry and some shots—that was when the news was passed back about the Regent. And there are gangs of roughs everywhere, so we thought we had better come home and make sure you were safe. I believe there was a lot of fighting in Old Palace Yard and I dare say it will spread.'

'Fighting in Old Palace Yard!' repeated Charlotte. 'But what will happen to Kit? And my father?'

Mary began to cry. Oswald, now rather conscience-striken, said unconvincingly that he didn't suppose there was any cause for alarm.

Charlotte gripped the back of her chair, feeling ill with apprehension for Kit's safety. The shock had somehow affected the mild attack of indigestion she had been trying to ignore for the past half-hour. She really had quite a bad pain.

Edward appeared, still somewhat pale, and demanded what the din was about. When he heard, he at once became alert and competent.

'Don't worry, girls. I'll go and see what's up.'

Miss Plummer had been carefully watching Charlotte. 'I think it would be a good thing, my lord, if we were also to send for Lady Brancaster's doctor.'

Only then Charlotte realized she had started in labour.

The next hour was very uncomfortable. Miss Plummer and the midwife kept Charlotte company in her bedroom (her sisters had been excluded) but though her intermittent pains were quite severe she felt them simply as an annoying interruption—her anxiety for Kit was acting as a drug, and it was maddening to be dependent on all these stupid people for information; if only she could hurry down to Westminster herself, she would soon find out what was going on. The servant who had been sent for Sir Richard Croft came back to report that the doctor was out, nobody knew where.

'Oh, who cares about him?' exclaimed the expectant mother unreasonably.

Miss Plummer cared a good deal.

At last there was a great bang of the front door and then the sound of feet running up the stairs—not at all the approach of a distinguished physician attending a noble patient. Charlotte stumbled across the bedroom and almost fell into Kit's arms as he came in.

'Oh, my darling—you're safe!'

'Well, why shouldn't I be? You're the one who's having the baby!'

'But they said there was fighting—is it true the Regent has been murdered?'

'Good heavens, no! Someone threw a stone

at his coach and broke the window, that's all. And there are hundreds of people milling about the streets, which is why I took so long to get home. But never mind that now—it is you I want to hear about. Do you feel very bad, my poor love? Where is that damned leech? He has no business to be out when my wife needs him!'

Sir Richard Croft arrived three hours later, full of apologies. Charlotte's son had been successfully delivered twenty minutes earlier by the midwife.

Charlotte lay in her warm, bright bedroom for the next fortnight, surrounded by care and affection, admiring visitors, letters of congratulation, flowering plants in pots and embroidered caps for the baby. Young Lord Willingale nestled in his cradle beside her, perfect in every respect, with Kit's grey eyes and long dark lashes.

No one intruded on her joy by speaking of the unpleasant things that were happening in the world outside. The attack on the Prince Regent had thrown the Government into a panic. They were convinced he had been shot at. Many people believed that his window had simply been broken by a random stone, and the episode came to be known derisively as the Pop-Gun Plot, but Lord Liverpool was taking no chances. He thought a revolution was about to break out and was getting ready to suspend Habeas Corpus, so that Radicals and reformers could be locked up without trial.

While Charlotte was still in bed, Kit was obliged to go and inspect some of his property in the Midlands. When he came back, he seemed tired and rather withdrawn, quite unlike himself.

'You must have had a wretched journey,' said Charlotte sympathetically. 'It's horrid travelling in winter.'

'The roads weren't too bad. Some of the people and places I visited—' He broke off, gazing at his wife and son. 'How good it is to be back here with you. So peaceful and serene.'

'Yes, but what were you going to say just now?'

'Oh, nothing important. Nothing to concern you, my love. Only that we are living in troubled times, and it is a great misfortune that the country should be managed at this moment by the two worst Prime Ministers since Lord North.'

What could he mean? Surely it was not possible to have more than one Prime Minister? She knew Lord Liverpool, of course (a fussy, well-meaning man). But who was the other?

'Lord Sidmouth,' said Kit. 'He is Home Secretary now, but years ago when he was plain Henry Addington he replaced Mr Pitt for a short time and nearly succeeded in losing the war.'

She remembered a couplet from her childhood:

> What Pitt is to Addington
> London is to Paddington.

She had imagined it was a nursery rhyme. And thinking of nursery rhymes, her attention returned to the much more fascinating subject of dear little Will.

They had decided to call him Will as an abbreviation of Willingale, which was his courtesy title. He was being given the name Christopher, like all the Colbrook eldest sons since Queen Elizabeth's reign. As soon as she was fit to travel, Kit took Charlotte and Will down to Essex for some country air. There was great rejoicing and lighting of bonfires on the estate—no signs of revolution in this corner of England.

CHAPTER FIVE

The young Marchioness of Brancaster was now able to take her proper place in society for the first time. She was nearly nineteen, she had been married for a year and a half, but her early marriage, followed by a long wedding tour and then her pregnancy, had kept her out of the Mayfair drawing-rooms. Now she was petted and fêted everywhere; it was the fashion to think her as beautiful as her mother—well, not so classically beautiful perhaps, but such a spirited creature, with so much vivacity and charm.

Charlotte enjoyed herself tremendously. There was so much to do. Delicious shopping expeditions, paying and receiving calls—she had thought this would be deadly, but it was nothing of the kind: at the house of one congenial friend you would meet half a dozen others, there would be much agreeable conversation and perhaps some plan made for the rest of the day, a visit to the Royal Academy, a trip to Battersea to see a steam engine. It was part of the ritual to drive in the park before dinner, and then there was the chosen amusement of the evening: the play or the opera, a reception or a ball.

Kit and Charlotte paid a weekly visit to his grandmother, old Lady Brancaster, at her house in Curzon Street. It was like stepping back half a century, for all the furniture was arranged formally round the walls with an open space in the middle of the room. The carved chair legs bent heavily outwards, so that they looked like stiff old men with swollen knees.

'And what are your engagements for today?' the old lady would ask. 'Where do you dine this evening?'

'At Melbourne House, ma'am,' Charlotte had to admit on one occasion.

'Consorting with a parcel of Whigs!'

'Whigs are so very amusing, I don't know why.'

'They've been in opposition a long time,' said Kit, 'and that gives them a good deal to be amusing about. Don't look so disapproving, my dear ma'am. I'm sure you never allowed politics to interfere with pleasure.'

It was Charlotte's private opinion that politics did interfere with pleasure far too often. Not at the mixed gatherings where everyone met on equal terms; here the bitter feuds of Westminster were tactfully ignored, which was one of the reasons she liked visiting Whig houses. The endless discussions began when all those present belonged to the same party.

The guests at Lady St Eudo's dinner, a few evenings later, were all hereditary Tories.

'Charlotte, my dear child, how charming you look,' said Lord St Eudo, coming forward to greet them.

He had been her mother's lover so long that he behaved to Charlotte as though he was some kind of uncle, and she almost expected him to pat her on the head. She was mildly fond of him but sensed that Kit was not.

'Ah, Brancaster,' said Lord St Eudo.

'My lord,' said Kit formally.

Lady St Eudo was a glacial woman who displayed no emotion of any kind. People had never found it hard to imagine why her husband was entralled by the tender-hearted sensibility of Aimée Rivers.

Charlotte took a quick glance round the room: there were eight other guests, including her cousin Olivia Chance, with Mr Chance looking ministerial, and a young couple called Rendal. She was by far the youngest person there. Sally Rendal was about twenty-six and everyone else between thirty and fifty. She was getting used to this, though she found it rather a strain. However, she had a prettier dress than any of the other ladies—a rose coloured gauze striped in gold, and worn with pearl and ruby ornaments.

Two of the men immediately started talking to her.

They went in to dinner. Charlotte was seated between her host and Mr Rendal, who wanted to know what she thought of a play they had both seen last week.

Everyone else was talking politics. Not, at first, the great issues of the day. It was the uual stuff: if Lord So-and-So were to resign his post, would Mr Such-and-Such be invited to replace him? But presently the gloomy state of the nation cast its shadow. Mr Chance was holding forth. '. . . I said to the Prime Minister, "if you want my advice . . ."'

Mr Rendal winked at Charlotte and she nearly exploded into laughter and social disgrace.

'As I was saying to Castlereagh only yesterday, we are in the same parlous condition as the French in 1789. The labouring classes seem to have lost what little sense they possess.'

'It may be rather difficult to remain level-headed,' said Kit's cool voice, 'when one is on the brink of starvation.'

'Starvation? Nonsense!' boomed Mr Chance. 'Nobody is starving.'

There was an awkward silence. The turtle soup had been replaced with a fine salmon, gleaming rosily on its bed of lettuce. A saddle of lamb dominated one end of the table, a roast peacock the other. Tureens of new potatoes and young peas, trays of asparagus, alternated with the side-dishes: a fricando of veal, kidneys in rice. A rich blend of savoury scents, laced with herbs and spices, rose from the beautiful dinner service, each piece painted with a different English landscape. And Mr Chance repeated aggressively that nobody was starving.

'A certain amount of hardship is always inevitable,' said St Eudo, with the air of making a concession. 'What do you propose one should do about it?'

Kit said, 'I think we ought to repeal the Corn Laws.'

There was an immediate outcry. All the men started talking at once and Lady Olivia joined in.

'My dear Brancaster—you cannot be serious!'

Even Charlotte understood why they were upset. The Corn Laws existed to control the import of foreign grain into England. Owing to the rise in prices during the war, it cost more to produce a load of bread than ever before. A supply of cheap corn from the Continent would be disastrous for the English farmers and their landlords.

'We should be ruined,' said someone.

51

Olivia, dressing up the idea more acceptably, said: 'The farmers would be ruined. They would not be able to pay their rents.'

'Then perhaps we should remit their rents,' said Kit.

Nobody was at all pleased by this suggestion.

One of the men said audibly to his neighbour, 'The Marquess is uncommonly generous. Do you suppose there are many acres under the plough in Hartwood Square?'

Kit flushed. He was the richest man in the room, and though he owned a great deal of agricultural land, much of his income came from the London property, where his well-to-do tenants were naturally unaffected by the Corn Laws.

'I realize that is not a solution,' he said. 'Many landlords could not survive without their present rents and there are plenty of independent farmers who have sunk their savings in buying land and stock. I believe the Government should float a loan to help these people, so that they could afford to take less for their wheat and still make a living. Then the Corn Laws could safely be repealed, bread would be cheaper, and prices in general would fall.'

For some reason they were more indignant than ever. Names like Malthus and Adam

Smith flew through the air. They seemed to be accusing Kit of some shocking crime. He could not have caused more alarm if he had repudiated the Thirty-Nine Articles.

Charlotte sat stiffly defiant, wanting to support him yet not knowing what to say. She admired his self-possession. He was the only person in the room, apart from Lady St Eudo, who appeared totally unmoved by the storm he was creating. Lady St Eudo was too well bred to admit that anything unusual was happening at her dinner-table.

The second course was served and eaten automatically. There was a fantastic dessert of spun sugar and almond cream that no one tasted. Charlotte would have liked a helping, but thought it would look heartless and greedy to eat it while her husband was being attacked by his intolerant friends.

Lady St Eudo collected the female guests and bore them upstairs to her sedate drawing-room, leaving the men to their port. This was not very comfortable for Charlotte either. Her cousin Olivia tried to get her in a corner to talk about Kit's strange behaviour—what was the matter with him? Was he ill? Charlotte was determined not to discuss her husband with his former mistress. Two of the other women stared at her resentfully and whispered, while their hostess conversed in

53

platitudes as though she was talking to herself. Only Mrs Rendal was friendly and natural.

At last the men began to drift back to the drawing-room in ones and twos, Kit being the first to arrive. Then there was a longish hiatus before their carriage was announced and they were finally able to escape.

'My dearest girl, I am so very sorry,' he said, as soon as they were shut up alone together in the carriage. 'You have had a most unpleasant dinner. That's the worst of having been a bachelor so long—I forget I have someone else's comfort to consider!'

'It does not signify. Tell me, where did you find these people who are starving? Was it when you went up to Warwickshire, just after Will was born?'

'I saw some horrifying sights, I had no idea things were so bad—or that they could be so bad, in a civilized country.'

'How dreadful,' said Charlotte. Inadequately, because she could not quite stretch her mind to imagine the conditions which he apparently did not wish to describe.

They were going on to a reception in St James's Square, and were now driving down Park Lane. The Park looked rural, almost wild, in the violet dusk. Once they turned into Piccadilly the high, bright light of the new gas lamps poured into the carriage, sharp and enquiring.

'Naturally I am doing everything I can to help and protect our own tenants,' he said. 'But this is a drop in the ocean. The greatest private fortune could not meet the need. That is why I think the Government should act.'

'Why were they all so cross when you suggested a loan to help the farmers? It sounded very sensible to me.'

'Yes, but it is a heresy, directly opposed to the economic law laid down in *The Wealth of Nations* by their great oracle Adam Smith. He thought that self-interest was the right and only spur to prosperity, that wealth must be allowed to find its own level, and that any interference with natural cause and effect must lead to national disaster.'

'How did he know?' asked Charlotte. And not waiting for an answer, 'Who was the other man they kept quoting? The one with the odd name?'

'The Reverend Doctor Malthus? Oh, he is a parson who has taken to mathematics.' Kit's voice was clipped with sarcasm. 'He thinks the population is bound to increase too fast, because he has noticed that when two people marry they often have eight or ten children.'

'A good many of them die in infancy.'

'Far fewer, since vaccination has reduced the danger of smallpox. However, the worthy Malthus has an excellent scheme for a new Act which would keep down the numbers of the indigent poor. When they apply for parish relief, no extra allowance should be made in respect of their children.'

'He would let them die of hunger?'

'He considers they ought not to be conceived.'

It took her a few seconds to work out the implications of this extraordinary doctrine.

'But that is to say that married people must not—that if we are poor we should not be able to make love!'

'Iniquitous, isn't it?' said Kit, who did not seem to mind the suggestion that they themselves might have been paupers, which would certainly have shocked the Chances or the St Eudos.

'He must be abominably stupid as well as wicked,' she said. 'As though anyone who was in love would pay attention to such a law!'

'I don't think he expects to be taken quite literally. He is like all these well-meaning wiseacres who try to frighten us out of our good instincts by prophesying doom.'

CHAPTER SIX

Kit continued to attack the supporters of
Adam Smith, in the House of Lords and else-
where. His Tory friends called him a Whig
and the Whigs called him a Radical. He
insisted that he was simply a dissatisfied
Tory. Charlotte naturally took his side and
accepted all his opinions without really understanding them. Though her enthusiasm
began to wane a little when she found their
social life being affected. He announced one
morning that he was engaged to dine and
spend the evening at the house of a well-
known banker.

'I am hoping he may be prepared to put up
some money towards a loan for the farmers.
It's plain the Government want nothing to do
with my ideas, so I shall try to interest some
commercial men instead.'

'Surely you need not go this evening? Have
you forgotten it's Wednesday?'

Wednesday was the night of the weekly
ball at Almack's, and she expected him to
postpone his meeting with the banker. She
was chagrined to find that he had no intention of doing so.

'You will have to send back the tickets and

say you are not well.'

'Send back the tickets! of course I can do no such thing!'

'Why not?' he asked, amused by her outraged expression. 'My darling, you don't mind missing Almack's for once? Think how you used to despise the place. Why, you married me to avoid going there!'

'What a shameless liar you are,' she said, laughing in spite of herself. 'I didn't want to be put on show with all the other husband-hunting girls, it's very different going as a married lady. Which reminds me, I must be there tonight because Mama has a cold, and I promised her I'd chaperon my sisters.'

'Then Edward can go with you. And I'll send a message round to Gerard and put him in charge of the expedition; you'll be quite comfortable with him to take care of you.'

Their country neighbour Gerard Winton was, in London, a most sought-after bachelor and very good company. If Kit would not come himself, he had at least chosen a substitute who would keep her entertained.

Charlotte, Edward and Gerard drove to Berkeley Street and collected Amelia and Mary Rivers. Amelia was now twenty-one, no longer frightened of going out in society, but still more serious than her married sister, as well as being two years older, so it was rather ridiculous that Charlotte had to act as her chaperon. However Amelia took this in good part. Mary had grown into a tall, handsome girl, anything but shy.

The weekly subscription balls at Almack's Rooms in King Street, St James's, were the pivot of fashionable life. No one could attend unless personally known to one of the patronesses. When Charlotte's party entered the famous blue ballroom, the ring of well-bred voices was reverberating back off the ceiling and everyone was complaining that it was a shocking squeeze. Yet they would not have had it otherwise, moving through the throng as though they were already engaged in some ritual dance, greeting friend and foe alike with equal courtesy. Most of her acquaintances asked Charlotte how her mother was, and where was Lord Brancaster this evening? She took great pains to answer the first question in order to slur over the second.

The band struck up a waltz and a young officer came to ask Mary to dance with him. Mary shot a challenging glance at Charlotte.

'My sister does not waltz, Captain Ridley, as I'm sure you know.'

Mary looked sulky, and Charlotte decided that this was a conspiracy between them, in the hope that she would not take her duties seriously.

'You, on the other hand, waltz admirably,' murmured Gerard, who was standing beside her. 'May I have the honour?'

'Not this evening, thank you. I ought to stay with my sisters while they are not dancing.'

In any case, the partner she wanted was Kit who had taught her to waltz in Paris on their honeymoon. A quadrille was different. Sets were made up as soon as the waltz was over, and once Amelia and Mary had partners, she took Gerard's arm and let him lead her on to the floor. Quadrille-dancing had become extremely popular. Instead of prancing up and down the whole length of the room and jostling with strangers, the dancers formed circles, four couples in each, and performed all the figures within their own set. It was very agreeable.

'How beautiful you look,' Gerard said to her while they were dancing. 'Kit must be mad to let you come here without him.'

As this was more or less what Charlotte thought herself, she gave him a glance of gratitude and approval that was quite dazzling. Out of the corner of her eye she saw Mrs Rendal, who was also in their set, looking interested. She immediately tried to seem unconcerned. Sally Rendal, now a great friend of hers, was the heroine of a good many sentimental adventures and could not see a woman smile at a man without hoping they were in love.

When the dance was over, Gerard led Charlotte towards two chairs comfortably drawn into a corner. She looked round conscientiously to make sure her sisters did not need her. Really, it was quite hard to make them out among so many girls in white with flowers in their hair and smiles on their faces, all hoping to be danced with, and if possible fallen in love with, by eligible men. Many of them were older than Charlotte, some had been coming to Almack's for five or six years. Amelia was happily talking to some friends of their mother's and Mary was with Edward. Charlotte could attend to Gerard.

He astonished her by saying, 'May I make a rather impertinent suggestion, Lady Brancaster?'

Good heavens, what could he mean? Was he going to tell her she ought not to be wearing emeralds with that particular shade of yellow? Or was it something far more personal? She had always been a little daunted by this contemporary of her husband, with his faintly supercilious good looks and critical glance.

'Please do,' she said, in some trepidation. 'I mean, please make your suggestion, and I 'will tell you if it is too impertinent.'

'Perhaps interfering is the word I want. I was wondering if you could restrain Kit from making all this outcry about the Corn Laws.'

'Restrain him? Why should I?'

'There, I have offended you. I was afraid I might.'

'No, not at all. I was rather surprised, that is all.'

'You must be aware that his views are highly unpopular.'

'Oh yes, with stuffy people like Mr Chance. But you are Kit's friend—'

'That's why I don't want him to injure his reputation as a sensible man, by annoying and upsetting the Ministers.'

'Don't you think he is right in wanting to bring down the price of bread?'

'It's more complicated than that. The country is in a very unsettled state and I'm afraid it is always the weakest who suffer most at these times. Naturally we must all do what we ought in the way of charity. And Kit does a great deal—he is very much loved and respected down in Essex, you know. Why can't he be content with that? He knows nothing of political theory, he was never interested until recently.'

Charlotte, having married for love at seventeen, had gone around happily imagining that her husband knew everything about everything.

'Do you remember,' Gerard continued, 'the day we first met in Italy? Kit told you that I represented his family borough, and that he expected me to say in the Commons what he was too lazy to say in the Lords. He was joking of course, but it was more or less true. Mind you, he is a very clever fellow— has a first-rate mind—and I think that is the danger. He takes up a subject and wants to master it straight away.'

It was late when Charlotte got home from the ball but Kit had only just returned. She was in bed, having dismissed her maid, when he came in from his room next door.

'How was your evening, my love?'

'Passable. How was yours? Did you get the money you wanted?'

'I'm not sure. He's thinking it over.'

Charlotte was sitting up in bed wearing a clear muslin nightdress so fine that it was literally transparent. The bed was extremely magnificent and had been specially designed for them by Wyatt. It was up three steps and stood sideways to the wall in a deep recess. Crimson curtains lined with sky blue hung straight down from the ceiling, where they were suspended from a tracery of Gothic arches. When they first saw this contraption

Kit had said it was a little like Westminster Abbey. However, the rather tactless resemblance to a tomb had never affected their sleep or their lovemaking.

He sat down on the edge of the bed and kissed her. He was wearing a dressing-gown of dark blue silk and looked rather medieval himself. She had caught a note of disappointment in his voice when he spoke of his meeting with the banker, and she thought this was an opportunity to be diplomatic.

'Kit, are you sure that what you are trying to do is wise?'

He stopped kissing her and held her a little away from him, gazing into her face with an amused speculation.

'Now who the devil has been talking to you and at Almack's, of all places? Olivia? Or that old fox St Eudo, was he there? But of course—it was Gerard! Can't bear to think I have any views that he doesn't manipulate. How tedious for you, my poor Char, to be bored to death by politics at a ball.'

She was annoyed with herself for having been obvious.

'I may not know anything about politics, but I can't help noticing when so many of our friends disagree with you. I don't wish to sound disloyal—'

'But you think I may be making a fool of

myself. Yet even if our condescending friends are right, and my ideas all wrong, I am at least trying to help some of those unfortunate people who have hardly any hope of better times. Surely you don't consider that a waste of effort?'

'Of course not. I am very sorry there is so much hardship,' she began automatically, and then stopped, wondering if this was true.

One was always being told about the dreadful smoky manufactories and the over-worked hands, toiling long hours and living in rows of nightmare hovels under the black chimneys. She had never visited such places or such alien communities and they had no reality for her.

'I suppose it is heartless of me, but I cannot feel for them as I ought. I don't see how we can alter their lot; my father says they choose to work in the mills because they can earn more money than they used to, and then they spend it on gin. And altogether they seem to me as far off and strange as the inhabitants of India or China.'

He said slowly, 'There is great poverty in the countryside too.'

Now she knew he was exaggerating. She had lived in the country all her life, and ridden about her father's estate at Clutton, knowing all the cottagers by name. They had snug houses and pretty gardens, kept chickens and geese and bees. They worked hard but lived well. If any family was overtaken by disaster, her mother would send help to them, and often found that everything necessary was already being done by their neighbours. It was the same story at Hartwood and among the Chances' tenants at Leavening.

'You are not convinced,' he said.

She did not want to argue, and said stiltedly, 'It is very good of you to spend so much of your time working for others.'

'My dear Char, you need not put up a statue to me! I am interested in what I'm doing; it's no sacrifice, I assure you. I always meant to make certain changes when I married. I needed some better occupation than sauntering down Bond Street or paying morning calls. And I've had fourteen years of Almack's, after all.'

But I haven't! The silent protest welled up inside her. How could he be so selfish? Didn't he know how much she enjoyed the pleasures he now affected to despise? And that she could only appreciate them properly if they were shared with him? If he wanted a wife who was ready to retire from the world, he would have done better to marry one of those vestal virgins who had spent several seasons at Almack's and who would probably have been only too thankful to see the last of the place.

'Several of your old flames were there this evening,' she said, apparently at a tangent. 'All very pretty and accomplished. Why didn't you marry one of them?'

'Don't be silly,' he said. 'I have told you a hundred times that you are the only girl I have ever seriously wanted to marry.'

Which was irresistible, though it left them at cross-purposes.

CHAPTER SEVEN

The Brancasters set out from London in mid-July to spend the summer at Hartwood. An impressive cavalcade wound its way northwards out of the great square: Lord and Lady Brancaster in one curricle (the Marquess driving), Lord Edward in another, Lord Oswald and Lord Hector on horseback, the travelling chariot occupied by Lord Willingale and his nurse, the town coach containing some of the upper servants, the second chaise transporting the family plate and guarded by the under-butler with a blunderbuss and four more stout fellows, a troop of grooms riding and leading the remaining saddle-horses, and three wagons in which the lesser servants sat on the baggage.

As they drove through the suburban cluster of Gothic villas and flowery gardens, many people turned to gaze at this almost royal procession.

In August Charlotte welcomed her first house-party. It was delightful to be Kit's hostess at Hartwood and she was proud of her own small contribution to the beauties of the place: an Inigo Jones colonnade which ran along one side of the house had now been glazed like an orangery against the biting Essex winds, and stone urns of fuchsias, hibiscus and geraniums were charmingly grouped round a collection of marble statues. The colonnade garden was her own idea and voted a great success.

It was the finest summer for several years and they made the most of it, with picnics in the forest, sketching parties, curricle races, a trip to see a ruined abbey, a cricket match. In the evenings they played charades and other games, or sometimes danced.

'I never enjoyed myself more at any country house,' declared Charlotte's particular friend Sally Rendal the day she was leaving. 'Belvoir and Bowood will have to look to their laurels. I hope we shall be meeting, by the way, at some other houses during the winter?'

'I'm not sure.' Charlotte hesitated. 'Kit says he does not mind how many people we have staying here, he enjoys it, but he gets bored visiting other people. I'm afraid it sounds dreadfully arrogant.'

'Well, if ever anyone had an excuse to be arrogant, it must be Lord Brancaster. If this place belonged to me I would never want to leave it. Only you must not allow yourself to become complete hermits, my dearest Char. It would be too dismal if none of your friends was to see you again until we are all back in London. Promise me that you will make him bring you to West Park, if we are able to get the builders out this side of Christmas.'

Charlotte promised readily, though not thinking anything would come of this invitation. Sally had talked a good deal about the inconvenience of having improvements made at their house in Berkshire, but Kit had explained to her privately that the Rendals' plans were always rather unsettled owing to Rupert Rendal's debts.

Although Kit said he had no intention of frittering away his time on a round of visits, he took his wife and son to stay with her parents in Surrey towards the end of September. He remained with them for nearly a month, then set off alone to make a tour of his property in the Midlands, leaving Charlotte and the baby to spend an extra fortnight with her family. Towards the middle of the second week she received a letter saying that he meant to extend his journey, he was finding so much to interest him, and she would therefore arrive home before he did. He was sure his dearest Charlotte would understand.

She was extremely disappointed. She was missing him a good deal and she immediately began to feel neglected and ill-used. Without much enthusiasm she turned to another letter that had come by the same post. It was from Sally Rendal.

Sally wrote to say that their house had just been made habitable; she and Rupert were hoping to assemble a few of their friends next week. (He must have backed all the right horses at Newmarket, thought Charlotte, reading on.) With apologies for the notice, Sally invited the Brancasters to join their party.

'Oh, it is too bad,' exclaimed Charlotte. 'The one house I wanted to go to, and Kit is not here!'

But did it matter? Couldn't she go alone, to close friends like the Rendals? She had her own carriage and servants with her, they could convey her to West Park, an easy distance of about fifty miles.

Her parents were a little perturbed when they heard her plan, but they could hardly prevent her going to Berkshire. She was a married woman now, and there was nothing definitely improper in what she wanted to do. Besides, Lady Rivers was bribed into complicity by the prospect of keeping her grandson a little longer in Surrey. Lord Rivers felt obliged to ask whether Charlotte was quite certain Brancaster would not object to her paying this unaccompanied visit.

'I promise you, Papa, Kit will not mind in the least,' she told him airily.

She told herself that she did not care whether he minded or not.

West Park was near Maidenhead, about a mile off the Bath Road. It was a large white house with Ionic pillars and a high portico; Rupert Rendal had inherited the place from an uncle without enough money to keep it up. Though no one would have guessed, thought Charlotte, as she was conducted through warm, freshly painted rooms, all with bright new carpets, prettily draped curtains and glossy modern furniture.

The Rendals were delighted to see her and the whole house-party combined to make a fuss of her, as though there was something daring and intrepid about travelling from Surrey to Berkshire in a private chaise with her own servants. Charlotte thought this very silly, though she was pleased to find that she knew all the other guests, including some distant cousins of Kit's, Mrs Breton and her daughter Virgilia, who had stayed with them at Hartwood in the summer. And Gerard Winton was there, remaining a little in the background and looking grave.

'I have put you next to Winton,' said Sally in her matter-of-fact way, escorting Charlotte to her room. 'I take it that is what you wanted.'

'Good heavens, no!' protested Charlotte, embarrassed and annoyed, yet obscurely flattered. 'You know very well he's not my lover. I don't have a lover. I am in love with my husband, the wretch.'

'Very proper sentiments,' said Sally, smiling. 'And if you change your mind, I promise not to tease you.'

After this Charlotte took care to keep away from Gerard. She spent the first evening flirting agreeably with her host, but this would not do; his current mistress was also staying in the house. She decided she must choose an unattached man to be her escort for the period of her visit, and after some careful observation (to avoid interfering with any preference of Sally's) she took up with a good-humoured if rather conceited young buck called Tom Danby, who was very willing to squire her about in the most gallant way.

Charlotte thought she had been rather clever in side-stepping Sally's attempt to link her with Gerard, so she was not very pleased the following afternoon when he cornered in in the conservatory, and said, 'I want to talk to you.'

'What about?' she asked, not very graciously.

'Your coming to West Park has caused a good deal of comment. Does Brancaster know you are here?'

'I don't see what that has to do with you, Mr Winton.'

He said something about being Kit's friend. 'I cannot help offering you a word of warning, Lady Brancaster, even if it offends you. Since you are here without your husband, you ought to be extrememly careful not to encourage a man like Danby, who will certainly jump to the wrong conclusion.'

'You are imagining—'

'No, I'm not. You've been leading him on for the last two days, I can't think why.'

She could not tell him, so she pretended to be very interested in one of Sally's exotic plants, which had a twisted stem and pale, hairy leaves (really, the poor thing looked quite sickly) and said over her shoulder, 'I am very well able to look after myself. And let me tell you, sir, Kit is not always lecturing me on how to behave. He does not care what I do.'

'If you think that,' said Gerard Winton frankly, 'you must be extremely simple-minded.'

Charlotte felt herself blushing, and was aware that they were completely exposed in a glass box. On one side of them, several of the

74

Rendals' guests were strolling in the garden, on the other side a group was seated in the drawing-room which lay behind the conservatory—it was the last place to have an argument with the man who had been singled out by Sally to become her lover. She brushed past him and went into the house.

It was odious of Gerard to suggest that she would not be able to keep Tom Danby in order, but during the evening she made the unfortunate discovery that he was right. Danby sat next to her at dinner, drank a good deal, and soon became amorous. He was a sturdily built man with thick brown hair, light brown eyes and a high colour. His incipient swagger had not worried her before; now it was accompanied by an incipient leer.

Presently the ladies were able to leave the table, but that was no escape; Mr Danby was the first man out of the dining-room and placed himself firmly at her side. She looked hopefully towards her hostess for rescue. Sally seemed to find the situation a very good joke. When they divided into teams to play charades—the popular craze—Charlotte and Danby were in the same team. Their turn for acting came and they all trooped out into the hall.

The word suggested was diplomacy. Half the players wanted to do it, the others said it was too difficult.

'How are we supposed to illustrate diplomacy in dumb-show?'

'That's easy. The Congress of Vienna—people round a table waving their arms and pretending to make speeches.'

'Or dancing waltzes.'

'The syllables will be quite simple. Dip (taking a dip at Brighton, you know), low, ma and sea. . . .'

The first three syllables were performed successfully. When they came to 'sea' it was harder to think of a mime, as everyone had already bathed so energetically at the beginning of the word.

'We'll have to have some boats.'

Pushing up a sofa from the far end of the drawingroom, Danby invited Charlotte to sit down on it and put her feet up, then he fetched a second sofa. They were a matching pair with high, curved ends; placed over the side and joined her, pretending to row. After a minute his hand slid down and she felt his fingers caressing her thigh.

Charlotte became rigid with anger. She was too inexperienced to know what she ought to do. She was not sure how much the others could see and she was afraid of provoking a scene which would make matters worse. So she sat stiffly, gazing ahead of her with a

76

frozen expression, while a flotilla of rugs and footstools assembled round their flagship.

As the scene ended, there was a plaintive enquiry from a lady in the audience who had not quite understood the rules.

'Do we have to guess now? Is it Antony and Cleopatra?'
ughter that followed did nothing to increase Charlotte's self-esteem.

She was thankful when it was possible to go to bed. Her maid Turnbull was waiting up for her. She helped Charlotte to undress and then retired. The house was silent, apart from the distant sounds of the gentlemen still carousing downstairs. Charlotte sat up in bed feeling lonely and disenchanted. She wished she had never come to West Park—if she had gone straight home, she might now have been lying in Kit's arms in their beautiful room overlooking the forest, instead of preparing to sleep alone in a house full of people who meant nothing to her.

There was a knock on the door.

'Come in,' she said, assuming it was Turnbull who had forgotten something, or Sally wanting to chat.

The person who came in was Tom Danby.

Charlotte gaped at him. 'What are you doing here? Go away at once!'

'No need for you to sound so outraged,

pretty Charlotte. Not a soul to hear you.'

The words were slurred, he was undoubtedly drunk, but he came on steadily towards the bed.

'How dare you come into my room!'

'I'd a notion I was expected. And any female who wears a shift like that is fairly begging some man to strip it off her,' added Tom Danby insolently, his hot brown eyes boring through her flimsy nightdress.

Charlotte dragged the quilt up to her chin. 'Don't touch me, you disgusting person, or I'll scream!'

'You'll cause a fine scandal if you do.'

The threat of a scandal checked her for an instant. He was now so close that she could smell the sweat and stale brandy that hung around his lurching body. What was she to do?

A furious voice from the doorway said, 'You touch her and I'll kill you!'

And Gerard was across the room, seizing Danby by the coat-collar and almost throttling him as he dragged him away from the bed. Danby kicked and spluttered, clutching at the air, but there was nothing he could do. Although he was taller and heavier than Gerard he was drunk and he had been taken by surprise. Gerard hustled him out of the room, cursing him savagely all the while, but in a whisper so as not to disturb the household. They disappeared into the passage.

Charlotte lay back against her pillows, acute relief mingled with dismay. She had certainly been saved from a very unpleasant encounter, but what must Gerard be thinking of her? She remembered him sitting in the front row during that unlucky charade, grim and unsmiling.

She heard his low voice outside the door. 'Lady Brancaster, may I come in?'

'Just one moment.'

She drew a shawl round her shoulders, remembering Tom Danby's remark about her nightdress. When Gerard came in with his fair hair ruffled and his cravat awry, she was looking eminently proper—or as proper as it was possible for a very pretty girl of nineteen to look, receiving a man in her bedroom at two in the morning.

They surveyed each other uneasily.

'How do you feel?' he asked. 'Do you need anything? Can I get your smelling-salts? You must have been so frightened. Though I think he was too drunk to—'

'To ravish me? I dare say, but it was very disagreeable all the same, and I do thank you for coming to my aid. I'm extremely grateful. What have you done with him?'

'Kicked him into his own room and left

him to cool off.'

'Oh. He won't try to call you out, will he?'

'Of course not. He hasn't a leg to stand on, and he'll realize that as soon as he sobers up.'

There was a short silence.

Fiddling with the fringe of her shawl, Charlotte said: 'I owe you an apology, Mr Winton. I must have behaved very stupidly if Danby thought I wanted him to make love to me. I hope you will not—that is—do you intend to say anything to Kit?'

'About this evening? Of course not. Unless you wish me to? I could reassure him that you were in no real danger. I hope you don't imagine I might tell malicious stories about you behind your back? I can promise you I won't. For one thing, Kit would probably knock me down, and for another, I'm not such a mean-spirited tale-bearer.'

He spoke so roughly that she was afraid she had insulted him by calling in question his masculine honour, which was as delicate as a woman's, though entirely different.

'You spoke as Kit's friend when you accused me of flirting with Danby—'

'Yes, and a damned piece of hypocrisy that was!'

She gazed at him in perplexity.

'I'm afraid I was perfectly indifferent to Kit's feelings, and anyway what the eye doesn't see, the heart doesn't grieve over. I was the one who suffered every time you fluttered your eyelids at that oaf. Because I'm in love with you myself and that's the truth—make what you will of it.'

She was completely taken by surprise.

'In love with me? I hadn't the smallest notion! How very interesting.'

He was rather put out by this remark, and then laughed. 'Interesting, indeed! You said that in exactly the same voice when we went to the British Museum and one of those learned fellows showed us the old manuscripts.'

'Oh dear, I did not mean to sound heartless, I beg your pardon. Only I cannot quite take it in—how long have you been thinking of me in this way?'

'Ever since the first day at Pompeii.'

'Good God! And I was quite afraid of your forming a bad impression. I was sure you had come to criticize.'

'Well, it's true that I had some forebodings when I heard Kit was to marry one of the Rivers girls—'

'Why, what did you think was wrong with the Rivers girls?'

'Oh, nothing,' he assured her hastily. 'Except that you were all very young. The minute I saw you together, I knew he had

81

been lucky beyond any man's deserts. And how the silly fellow can bear to be parted from you—'

'He is silly, isn't he?' said Charlotte lovingly. It seemed to her that she and Kit had both been fairly blind. Only one person had suspected Gerard's feelings. 'Did you know that Sally is always teasing me about you? That was the only reason I pretended to like Tom Danby. Because she made me feel so awkward.'

Somewhere in the house a clock chimed. Their compromising situation struck them both at the same moment.

'I mustn't stay here!' exclaimed Gerard. 'Good night, my dearest Char.'

He almost fled from the room.

CHAPTER EIGHT

Next day the men went out shooting, so Charlotte did not see either of her admirers during the morning, which gave her a little time to meditate and compose her thoughts. She had expected to stay awake for the rest of the night doing this, but in fact she had slept remarkably well. She found nothing but pleasure in the idea that Gerard was in love with her: a painless pleasure that warmed her without touching any of the deeper emotions that were all centred round Kit. The degrading episode with Tom Danby was quite overshadowed by this new discovery.

It was tiresome to have to stay indoors with the women and their endless chatter, their half-spiteful allusions to her conquests. About three in the afternoon she decided she would like to go out and meet the shooters on their way home. She could hardly set off alone, so she asked if anyone would care to come with her.

There were some amused glances which annoyed her, but most of the ladies drew closer to the fire.

'I'll come with you, Cousin Charlotte,' volunteered Virgilia Breton, jumping up with the pretty attentiveness of a young girl to a married lady—which was a little ridiculous as she was five years older than Charlotte.

Well wrapped up against the November frost, they took the path that Sally had pointed out to them. Virgilia's mother was a cousin of the Colbrooks; her father had made a fortune in some sort of unmentionable trade, so she was quite an heiress. She always made up to her titled relations, and did so now.

'What a charming bonnet . . . How well that colour suits you, my dear cousin . . . This is a pleasant prospect, but of course there is nothing here to compare with dear Hartwood. . . .'

Charlotte generally took people at their face value, but she could never quite believe that Virgilia really liked her.

An occasional shot rang out ahead of them, and the raucous voices of beaters shouting in a patch of woodland. They came to a stile and Charlotte stopped.

'Sally said we should wait for them here.'

Presently a figure came out of the wood. It was Tom Danby. Seeing them, he hesitated, then raised his hat in a salute and came eagerly to meet them.

I wonder he has effrontery, thought Charlotte. She did not wish for any embarrassing signs of contrition, still less for a formal apology, yet she really could not stomach the bumptious jocularity with which he came grinning towards her. Then she realized that this display of male fascination was not meant for her. He gave her the barest greeting and turned all his flattery on Virgilia.

'What, have you come specially to meet us, Miss Breton? I shall appoint myself your escort—as a reward for shooting the most pheasants.'

Virgilia preened and simpered, probably pleased to think she had captivated the man who yesterday had been running after Charlotte. This suited Charlotte, who was able to wait for Gerard. He came out of the wood, his gun under his arm and carrying a pheasant, limp in death but still with that metallic gleam of colour round the throat. His dog ran at his heels.

He smiled when he saw her and she fell into step beside him.

'Did you kill that poor creature?' she asked. 'How pretty the feathers are.'

'Scamp retrieved him and laid him at my feet. I've been too distracted all day to hit anything.'

The returning sportsmen, their dogs and loaders, struggled back towards the house. Gerard and Charlotte made a little detour through a shrubbery of evergreens. Out of sight of the others, he laid down his gun and the pheasant, took Charlotte in his arms and kissed her.

She made no effort to stop him. Observing her own sensations, she found it was very enjoyable to be kissed by Gerard Winton. And why not? If one could love only one man, there was surely no harm in liking another?

'I suppose you will say I should not have done that,' he remarked releasing her.

'You resisted temptation last night, when you ran away. It is far less improper out here in daylight.'

'It is just as improper,' he contradicted her. 'Only a good deal less dangerous.'

When they joined the rest of the party in the library, Charlotte's cheeks were tingling from excitement and the cold, crisp air and she was indifferent to what anyone might be thinking. Sally had just suggested that they should have an impromptu concert after dinner. They would all be obliged to perform. There were protests from her less talented guests.

'Nonsense, of course you can all do something,' she told them. 'Those who aren't musical must recite or show us a card trick.'

'I can stand on my head,' offered a young

Guards officer. 'Do it at guest nights. Will that suit?'

There was a clatter of horses in the drive outside and a private carriage swung past the library windows.

'Who the devil can be calling at this hour?' asked Rupert Rendal. 'We haven't invited anyone else to stay, have we, Sal?'

'I hope not, because there are no beds to spare.'

Everyone stood listening to the sounds of an arrival in the hall.

The butler opened the door and announced: 'The Marquess of Brancaster.'

Charlotte's heart gave a violent leap, apparently in two different directions. In a daze of confusion she watched Kit come in, dark and formidable, his face unsmiling, his grey eyes remote. He's found out, she thought immediately. But that was ridiculous. How could he possibly know that Tom Danby had burst into her bedroom last night, or that Gerard had just been kissing her in the shrubbery? He was hurt and unhappy because she had come gallivanting to West Park, instead of waiting at home for him like a loving wife. She began to feel guilty.

Sally greeted him with her usual engaging friendliness. 'How delightful that you are able to join us after all, Lord Brancaster. You have been very much missed, especially by your wife—Charlotte, where are you?'

Charlotte was propelled forward. He put a hand on her shoulder and gave her a decorous public kiss. She sensed that he was under a considerable strain, and when Rendal made a civil enquiry about his journey he did not reply, but stared around him at the assembled guests. Charlotte saw Tom Danby quaking slightly. She dared not look at Gerard.

Sally tried again. 'I dare say you and Charlotte want a little time to yourselves. We can put back dinner—'

'My dear Mrs Rendal, forgive me.' Kit recovered his poise. 'You must think me amazingly ill-mannered. The fact is, I heard some very shocking news an hour ago, and I was wondering whether it had reached you yet. I see it has not.'

'Good gracious, what has happened?'

'Princess Charlotte is dead.'

'Who told you so, my lord? Can it be true?'

'And what of the child?'

'The child was born dead. It was a boy. I was given the story the last time I changed horses and I fear it is undoubtedly true; a courier from Claremont had passed through some hours before, taking the news to the Queen, who is at Bath. The Regent is staying with the Hertfords.'

Everyone in that fashionable house-party had either met, or at least seen at close quarters, the Princess Charlotte of Wales, only daughter of the Prince Regent and heiress to the throne. Charlotte Brancaster remembered being taken as a child to play with the boisterous little girl who would one day be Queen of England, so she was told. And this summer, at balls and official receptions, she and Kit had several times exchanged a few words with the Princess and her young German husband. They had seemed blissfully happy.

'Poor Prince Leopold!' she exclaimed, her eyes filling with tears. 'What must he be feeling?'

'An utter desolation,' said Kit quietly.

As he glanced down at her, she knew he was remembering the birth of their own son nine months ago. She had even had the same doctor as the Princess—though young Will had outwitted Sir Richard Croft by arriving unexpectedly on the day of the Pop-Gun Plot.

When they went up to change, Kit saw the dress Turnbull had laid out for Charlotte: it was a clear shade of apple green, the gauze sleeves spangled with tiny beads of crystal.

'I'm afraid you cannot wear that, my love. You have no black with you, I suppose? Or

89

white would be the best alternative,'

'I have my white silk—but surely one is not expected to put on mourning at such short notice?'

'I think you'll find the other ladies do.'

And sure enough they all came down to dinner in black or white dresses, from some of which coloured trimmings had been hastily removed. There was no impromptu concert afterwards, no one felt at all frivolous and they sat round lamenting the Princess's death and wondering what was to happen now. None of the children of George III had legitimate heirs (plenty of illegitimate descendants, of course, and one could find some comic relief in trying to count the little Fitz-Clarences) but there was no one to step into Princess Charlotte's place, and in any case she was the only member of the Royal Family whom anyone cared two straws about. Her death would probably mean the end of the Monarchy.

'It's very sad,' said one the older ladies. 'Three years ago, when we defeated Bonaparte, we all looked forward to a time of peace and happiness. Now everything has gone wrong and England is on the verge of revolution. I don't understand why.'

It was late when Kit and Charlotte were finally alone in the bedroom where such odd things had happened the night before. She was now feeling rather conscience-stricken. Kit's sudden appearance, his actual presence and its violent impact on her senses, the news of a young woman's tragic death, which made the excitements of the last few days seem so trivial—all these things were having their effect on Charlotte, when she asked, a little nervously, 'Did you mind my coming here without you?'

'No, my darling: I'm not such a dog-in-the-manger. Though I wondered whether you might find a few pitfalls in the way of a solitary female guest at this kind of house-party. I was going to say booby-traps, only that is not very polite.'

'Well, I did accidentally raise Tom Danby's hopes a little, which I admit was a booby-ish thing to have done. However, he has now been completely disillusioned.'

'I am delighted to hear it,' said Kit, amused and apparently not considering it necessary to probe any further. 'And I should not have felt at all anxious about you, if I had known that Gerard was one of the party. He would always take care that you didn't get into a scrape.'

Charlotte stopped feeling guilty. At that moment she actually wanted to shake her husband for being so complacent. As he was happily unaware of this, he lay down beside her and drew her close, waking her with his hands and whispering their private love-names. Charlotte's chameleon emotions made another swift change.

CHAPTER NINE

Life was very quiet when they got back to Hartwood. They hunted two or three days a week, but there was no entertaining, owing to Court Mourning and the only neighbours they visited, ironically enough, were the Wintons.

Gerard's mother and his unmarried sister Letty lived with him in a moderate-sized brick house which Robert Adam had designed for his grandfather. They had no London house—Gerard occupied chambers in Half Moon Street. Mrs and Miss Winton did not aspire to move in the fashionable circles where he was a well-known figure, but they were agreeable, well-informed women and Kit was particularly fond of Mrs Winton who had been kind to him when he was a motherless little boy. He was always dropping in at Troughton House and expecting Charlotte to go with him. Once, when she tried to get out of it, he was quite sharp with her.

'I am sorry if the prospect bores you. The Winton ladies are better born than many of your London friends and infinitely better bred, even if they cannot keep up with the latest affectations and smart catch-phrases.'

Flushing resentfully, Charlotte was unable to defend herself. She did not wish to explain what she was really trying to avoid: the sight of Gerard dumb and suffering, his eyes following her about like a dog's. Declaring his love had apparently made it more painful. They had not been alone together since that afternoon in the shrubbery at West Park and Charlotte was not anxious for a meeting, her feelings were too ambiguous.

Kit did eventually notice that something was the matter with Gerard and jumped to the wrong conclusion.

'He doesn't approve of my taking an independent line over the Corn Laws.'

Charlotte did not enlighten him, though she could hardly have explained why. And when they all returned to town in January she was glad she had kept her mouth shut, for Kit plunged back wholeheartedly into his fight against the Corn Laws and she needed Gerard as an escort. It might not be very kind to make use of him—but he seemed delighted and his spirits revived immediately.

Kit was extremely preoccupied. He was coming to believe that the Corn Laws would only be abolished as part of a programme of general reform; he was still trying to float the loan he considered necessary to safeguard the farmers, and altogether he was too busy to take Charlotte to more than half the parties and entertainments they were expected to attend. Gerard took her to the rest.

Besides squiring her in public, he called on her nearly every day, and they had long interesting discussions, full of sympathy and feeling. In between the discussions Gerard tried to make love to her, as far as she would let him.

Gradually the interludes of dalliance became more frequent, so that Charlotte sometimes felt obliged to call a halt.

'You are behaving very badly, I wish you would stop.'

'How unconvincing you sound when you are trying to be moral. You only do it because you think you have to be a dutiful wife.'

'I'm not a dutiful wife—I mean, that isn't the reason I won't let you make love. I am perfectly content to be in love with Kit.' She was rather tired of being patronized by people older and more worldly than herself, so she added grandly: 'When I want to take a lover, I shan't be held back by any stuffy ideas about duty. I believe one should follow the desires of the heart.'

'Bravo!' said Gerard. 'So do I.'

They were in Charlotte's pretty upstair dressing-room, overlooking the square. She had gone to sit decorously on a straight chair, with her work-table in front of her as a fortification. They eyed each other, almost like enemies.

'I hope the desires of your heart will soon lead you in my direction,' he said hopefully. 'Considering the way Kit neglects you—'

'He doesn't! You have no right to say so, and I call it very shabby, the way you are always carping about him now; he has been a good friend to you.'

'I know, love,' said Gerard. 'I know I'm an ungrateful hound. Can't you understand what it feels like to be driven mad with jealousy?'

'No, I can't. I have never felt jealous in my life. I haven't a jealous nature.'

She spoke with finality. She had always been proud of her immunity from this vice. There was an incident in her early childhood which she could still just recall: at four years old she had gone with her parents and Amelia, who was then six, to visit some old maiden cousins in Kensington. These ladies had been expecting Lord and Lady Rivers to bring their eldest child with them, and they had bought her a most beautiful doll. They were not prepared for Charlotte and there was no present for her. She could remember seeing the doll given to Amelia and the

96

outrage of realizing there was nothing for her. She held back her roars of fury and dismay because she was already an advanced child who hated to be thought a baby. The old ladies were full of flustered apologies. And then her father had lifted her on to his knee, saying, 'She does not grudge her sister's pleasure. My good little Charlotte is never jealous.' This was better than a present—especially when one knew that kind Amelia would be willing to share the doll. And something in her father's voice had made Charlotte believe that the absence of envy or jealousy was a positive virtue.

So she was not very patient with Gerard.

'I wish he would not be so sorry for himself,' she said to her confidante Sally Rendal.

'Poor fellow, how cruel you are,' said Sally, laughing.

'I'm not sentimental, and neither are you,' retorted Charlotte. It was one of the things that had drawn her to Sally; neither of them had much use for soulful intensity. 'Be honest and admit that men who sulk are not romantic, they are simply tiresome; Gerard goes around looking so melancholy, it is quite absurd. And Kit still hasn't realized what is the matter with him.'

'Are you sure?' said Sally.

97

Charlotte stared at her. 'What are you suggesting? That Kit knows Gerard is trying to make me his mistress, and doesn't care?'

Sally shrugged. 'I expect he'd say that he cared if you asked him. It would be rather unchivalrous to say anything else. And besides, a man hates admitting anything that might reflect on his own virility. But when you come down to it, Char, what most husbands want is a wife who won't make scenes when they go off and leave her at home, and who will be charmingly good-tempered when they come back. How can they hope for that, unless we are allowed to have lovers?'

Charlotte knew this was how many married people behaved in their aristocratic circle— her own parents were a case in point. So that even if she did not happen to want an affair, she could hardly object because a very popular and sought-after bachelor insisted on being in love with her.

The cold, grey summer continued. Three of the Royal Dukes hurried into matrimony with German princesses. Kit's gushing cousin Virgilia Breton married Charlotte's former admirer Tom Danby; she thought them well matched.

In the middle of June the Brancasters held a large reception. Charlotte sent out three hundred cards; it was pleasing to hear that everyone in London society was dying to be asked.

On the morning of the great day, when the servants were turning the place upside down, Kit announced that there was a man he particularly wanted to see in connection with some newspaper articles. Charlotte was deciding what flowers she wanted to decorate the rooms and did not pay much attention. He set off in his curricle, dressed as though he was going out of town.

He did not come home to dinner at six o'clock. Charlotte took this fairly calmly, for the party was not due to start until half past ten, by which time it was hoped both Houses would have risen. When he was still missing at eight, she began to get restive.

'Where was he going?' asked Edward.

'I don't know—to see a stupid journalist or Radical or manufacturer, one of that set of vulgar persons he has forever hanging round the house,' said Charlotte, who was constantly irritated by the odd visitors she kept bumping into. She could have overlooked their humdrum appearance and unpolished accents, but they were all so deadly dull. 'I suppose he has clean forgotten the party.'

'Perhaps he's had an accident,' suggested Oswald, always dramatic.

'Don't be so gloomy, Oz,' said Edward, with an eye on Charlotte.

Charlotte, who was not a nervous girl, did not expect people to have accidents. She thought Kit's inconsiderate behaviour was all part of his wrong-headed obsession with tiresome matters that were no concern of his.

When there was no sign of him by ten o'clock, Edward asked, 'Would you like me to receive the guests with you, Char? If he is still not here?'

'Oh yes, please do,' she said gratefully.

The Rivers family had been invited to come early.

'You look very pretty, my dear,' Charlotte's father told her, adding complacently. 'I have a troop of uncommonly handsome women to be proud of.'

His wife was still the greatest beauty, but Amelia and Mary were looking their best. Each had a special interest in someone who would be at the party. Mary was in love with a young man called Giles Palmer, the heir to a Yorkshire baronetcy, while Amelia had a middle-aged suitor whose quiet tastes agreed with hers very well.

When they had all admired each other's dresses, Lady Rivers said, 'Where is Kit?'

'You may well ask,' replied Charlotte.

She was so cross that she left Edward to

explain. And he went on gallantly explaining, covering up for his half-brother, during the two hours that he spent standing next to her just inside the white and gold drawing-room.

'. . . I am deputizing for my brother, sir . . . my lady . . . your grace . . . asked to express his regrets . . . unavoidably detained . . .'

So that Charlotte had only to smile like a hostess and was not called on to invent excuses.

At last everyone was there, except the host, and then she had to move through the crowded rooms, pretending to enjoy herself. Eventually Oswald whispered to her that Kit was now in the house, he had gone straight off to change into evening dress, and very soon after that she caught the familiar sound of his voice behind her, apologizing to the Prime Minister.

'A driving mishap on a country road, my lord, and I could not get hold of another carriage for love or money.'

Charlotte felt her throat muscles tightening in anger and disbelief. She would not even look round. A moment later he was beside her.

'I'm so sorry, Char. Will you forgive me? We seem to be having a very successful party.'

101

'No thanks to you,' she said coldly.

Then they had to separate and circulate. At the end of the evening, when everyone was leaving, they stood together saying good night to the guests. At last the porter closed the front door behind the final reveller and the four Colbrooks were left to themselves.

'My God, I'm hungry!' exclaimed Kit. 'I never had any dinner.'

He fetched a plate of cold chicken and a bottle of champagne and took them into one of the small ante-rooms, followed by a footman carrying a tray of glasses and a dish of lobster patties.

The footman withdrew and Kit's relations gathered round to watch him pick up a chicken leg in his fingers and attack it with his strong, even teeth.

'Pour us all a glass of wine, Edward,' he said. 'I'm sure you deserve one after your exertions; I have been hearing on all sides what an excellent host you made. I knew I could rely on you.'

Edward looked absurdly gratified.

Charlotte said, 'I suppose that is why you found it unnecessary to put in an appearance until the evening was nearly over.'

'Char, he couldn't get home any earlier,' protested Oswald. 'There was an accident.'

'An accident!' repeated Charlotte scorn-

102

fully. She was maddened by the uncritical way Kit's brothers accepted everything he did or said, it was the last straw. 'If you believe in that accident, Oz, you must be as simple as all those Ministers we had here this evening, and you are always telling us how stupid *they* are. That mysterious accident was the best he could manage by way of an excuse for not troubling about a party in his own house. He doesn't care for the Ministers' consequence any more than he cares for our being left in the dark and made to look fools.'

'That is not true,' said Kit. 'My dear child, I know you have had a difficult evening and you are tired, but there is no need to twist everything out of all reason.'

On being called his dear child, Charlotte had a violent impulse to throw something at him. She looked round for a missile and her eye fell on the lobster patties.

'No, you don't!' said Kit hastily, putting out an arm to bar her away.

She tried to push him aside: he winced unexpectedly as she touched him and at the same moment she felt a slight bulge under his sleeve.

'What have you done to your arm?' she asked, breaking off in the middle of the temper she was deliberately fanning into a storm.

'It's only a scratch. I was thrown against a tree when the wheel came off the curricle.'

Charlotte stared at him in dismay. 'Do you mean there really was an accident?'

'Of course there was, you disbelieving little termagant.'

'Kit, how dreadful—you might have been killed! And I have been so cross and unkind.'

'Never mind, love,' he said gently, encircling her with his good arm as she pressed her face against his shoulder, overcome with remorse.

Oswald stood gaping at them until firmly led away by the more tactful Edward.

Presently Kit and Charlotte were seated on a small sofa, taking alternate sips of champagne out of the same glass.

'I don't blame you,' he said, 'for being exasperated by my performance tonight, but surely you were not serious when you accused me deliberately cutting the party? All other considerations apart, do you really imagine I could behave so insultingly to several hundred guests in our own house?'

Charlotte was confused. She knew she had been working up a grievance against him which she could not justify.

'It was stupid of me,' she admitted. 'I should have realized—only I never know what you will do next. You behave so differently from other people, everyone says so. When we married I thought I knew what it meant to be a member of the House of Lords. Papa simply goes down there to hear the debates and to vote. But your kind of politics seem to happen everywhere except Westminster and you are never here when I need you.'

'Poor Char, I'm sorry. If only I could make you see why . . .' He gazed down at her with those very intent grey eyes and met nothing but weariness and incomprehension. 'It's no use, is it? Try to bear with me a little longer and then we'll take a holiday. How would you like to go to Scotland?'

'To Scotland? When?

'Next month, when the boys go up to their mother as usual. You know she and Sir Robert have invited us to visit them whenever we choose.'

Kit's stepmother and her second husband lived in a castle beside a lake (which was called a loch). There was an island with a ruined chapel. There were mountains whose lofty crags overlooked deep glens and foaming torrents. The clansmen wore their native dress and spoke a strange, barbaric language. These descriptions from Oxwald and Hector sounded as though they came out of an unwritten *Waverley Novel* and Charlotte had also heard about the delightfully informal

105

pleasures of Highland house-parties.

'There is nothing I should like better,' she said, her eyes shining. 'I can hardly wait for July.'

But when July came, Kit said he must go to Manchester.

CHAPTER TEN

'To Manchester?' repeated Charlotte. 'What can you possibly want to do there?'

'Twenty thousand men are out on strike; jenny-spinners, power loom weavers, dyers and bricksetters—'

'I don't see what that has to do with you.'

'No, of course you don't, love—so let me explain. You know I have been trying to raise a loan to help the farmers bring down the price of grain; unluckily most of the wealthy manufacturers are such thorough townsmen, they cannot appreciate the difficulties of country people. But now these fellows in Manchester have their mills standing idle, their hands are striking for higher wages because they cannot afford to buy bread. I believe this would be a good moment to make some of the masters see that supporting the growers of English wheat might be their cheapest solution in the long run.'

Charlotte hardly listened to what he was saying. She simply stated: 'We are starting for Scotland on Monday.'

They had come down to Hartwood for a few days so that Kit could attend to some estate business. Oswald and Hector had already set out for the North; Edward was at Brighton and meant to follow soon. Will had been conveyed to his doting grandparents and aunts in Surrey.

'I am afraid we shall have to put off our trip for a week or two,' said Kit in a placating voice. 'It cannot signify, however.'

'Of course not. My wishes are not of the slightest importance, compared with the whims of the powerloom weavers.' Charlotte tried to sound ironic, but the words came out with an incipient whine. She added, unkindly, 'I wonder just how much your presence will signify to all these people you are so besotted about.'

There was a momentary expression in his eyes which she had never seen before, but he got up from the breakfast-table, where the argument was taking place, saying with his usual equanimity that he might as well start for Manchester that day.

He spent the morning making his arrangements; he had to see his agent and attend to various letters. Charlotte hung about, feeling useless and certain that Kit thought her frivolous and selfish. Then she had a brilliant idea—why shouldn't she go to Manchester with him? It sounded a horrid place but a strike might be rather exciting and they would be halfway to Scotland when his tiresome business was over.

Kit seemed rather touched by her offer, but firmly refused it.

'You would be bored to tears and there would be nowhere suitable for you to stay. Besides, there may very well be riots, and if you were with me I should not have a moment free from anxiety.'

'I don't see why,' complained Charlotte, her disappointment reinforced. 'Riots cannot be so very dangerous. If these people are all starving, as you say—'

'I did not say they were already starving. I said—'

'Oh yes, I know! It is the price of the quartern loaf—I beg of you, Kit, don't tell me any more about that old loaf. Does no one ever eat anything else?'

'Cake, for instance? My dear Char, are you trying to emulate Marie Antoinette?'

The fact that this was said lightly, as a joke, made it all the more intolerable. Charlotte was so angry that she could hardly bring herself to see him off with a decent show of affection. Pride prevented her from making a scene in front of the servants, but as soon as the carriage was out of sight she took herself into the Inigo Jones colonnade where she stamped up and down between the exotic plants and the marble statues, as she worked herself into a tremendous rage. And then, when she was ready to pour out her grievances, there was no one at Hartwood she could talk to.

There was, however, a suitable confidant within reach. Gerard was at Troughton House; she suspected he had come down on her account, for his mother and sister were away, taking the sea air at Ramsgate. She ordered her pony phaeton and set off to look for sympathy.

The shortest way to Troughton House was by a forest ride where the ground was too soft for heavy traffic. She soon had her ponies cantering over the chocolate-brown soil, the little phaeton leaping behind them as though it was a boat scudding over a rough sea. The tree-trunks rushed by, and far ahead at the other end of the ride she saw something bright and pale flashing in and out of the bars of sunlight. It was a man on a grey horse coming towards her.

She reined in the ponies. Halfway along the ride they met and came to a standstill.

'Oh, Gerard, I'm so unhappy!' cried Charlotte. 'What do you think he's done now?'

'Left you alone, the heartless brute, while he goes off on some wild-goose chase! It's altogether abominable!'

Gerard had met one of the Hartwood

grooms while he was on his morning ride, and had been told that his lordship had suddenly decided to go to Manchester. He was on his way to console Charlotte when they met. He dismounted and came to lift her out of the phaeton. She clung to him for comfort. Gerard petted and caressed her and called her his precious girl. Presently he went and tied up the horses. Then he took Charlotte's hand and led her a short distance away into a clearing where the bracken stood thick and green. He had brought a rug from the phaeton and spread it on the bracken, drawing Charlotte down beside him. She lay back, gazing up at him, her lips slightly parted, while he undid the buttons of her spencer. The gentle comforting changed into something quite different.

CHAPTER ELEVEN

I have taken a lover, thought Charlotte next morning, sitting at her dressing-table and staring into the glass. The hazel-green eyes gazed back at her, limpid and candid; her strongest feeling was one of surprise that she should feel so little. Surely she should have been mysteriously changed by the episode in the forest?

Once a woman was no longer a virgin, she was not going to be altered by the circumstance of making love. Probably this was why one's friends took such affairs in their stride, unlike the characters in plays and novels, with all their romantic agonizing. Perhaps this was why Sally had assured her that Kit would not mind.

But I want him to mind, thought Charlotte, who had rushed into Gerard's arms in order to pay Kit out for going to Manchester. Then she thought paradoxically, No, I don't. I don't even want him to know.

This was confusing and irrational; it took her some time to sort out. In the end she decided that she was not quite convinced by Sally's arguments, she had an idea that Kit would be hurt if he knew the truth. And she did not really wish to cause him pain.

Her maid Turnbull came in, bringing a letter on a salver. Charlotte recognized the writing: it was from Gerard. Turnbull probably knew this too, though of course she gave no sign. She had a large flat face and large flat feet and was quite unlike the pert, intriguing lady's maid of popular comedy.

Charlotte opened the letter and here she found herself confronted by a wave of romantic fervour.

Troughton House
Thursday

My adored Charlotte,
How to express in words the intense delight of loving each other as we did today! Oh my beautiful, gracious girl, this is all I have lived for since the day at West Park that I first held you in my arms . . .

Oh dear, thought Charlotte uncomfortably. Gerard was so much in love with her, and apparently he imagined that she was just as much in love with him. Which she was not. It was her own fault, she had encouraged him, she had responded with a frank desire for pleasure, and afterwards, when he was talking soulfully about ideal passions, she had found it impossible to tell him that she did

113

not entirely share his noble sentiments.

Perhaps it would be wiser and kinder to everyone if she brought their liaison to a still-born conclusion before it had properly begun.

Downstairs Hartwood was abominably dull. The rooms were too large and silent for one person to be in alone, and if she refused to admit how much she was missing Kit, she was certainly missing Will. Now eighteen months old, he was walking and talking and normally they spent delightful hours every day playing together.

She was nibbling a sandwich from her solitary luncheon tray when Mr Winton was announced. He had called, most correctly, to enquire after her health.

'And to make sure you are not moping while Brancaster is away,' he said cheerfully, for the benefit of the footman.

When they were alone he took both her hands and kissed them, holding them tight while he bent to kiss her mouth.

'Are you glad to see me, sweetheart?'

'Yes, of course. I have had such a stupid morning with no one to talk to. Do sit down and help me to eat these sandwiches.'

Gerard accepted a sandwich rather absently, drank a glass of marsala, and then tried to kiss her again. She shied away.

'Not here, Gerard. The servants—'

He let her go at once and moved away. 'I quite understand.'

Perhaps he thought she was uneasy with him in a place where Kit had stamped his presence so indelibly; this was the kind of sentimental irrelevance which might matter to him though not to her. Yet she admired his consideration and tact and she did find him attractive, with his fair, graceful good looks, his gentle manners. It was a pleasant change to be with someone so amenable, when one lived with a man who always got his own way.

'If you would care to go out,' he said, 'may I take you for a drive? I have my new curricle waiting.'

She could not resist this invitation, and while they were driving perhaps she could hint to him that he must not expect too much from her or let his feelings become too deeply engaged. But then it came on to rain when they were only half a mile from the house. Naturally he took her there to shelter. Troughton was peaceful and private; his mother and sister were away and the servants, making the most of this, were not on view. Soon Charlotte and Gerard were upstairs in his room. It was a good deal more comfortable than the bracken.

During the next week Charlotte drifted,

allowing Gerard to direct her actions because he knew his own mind much better than she knew hers. And because he could beguile and amuse her. Why should she deny herself an enjoyment that was doing nobody any harm? It could have no effect on her real life as Kit's wife and Will's mother. They were like an extended dream, those long, sensual afternoons in bed with Gerard. Afterwards one always had to get up and dress, a dismal anticlimax. She wondered, not for the first time, how her mother and St Eudo arranged the practical details of their long love affair. She had often wanted to ask, but Mama always avoided any sort of intimate discussion, even with a married daughter.

Charlotte heard a couple of times from Kit. In his second letter he said that the strikers were parading through the streets of Manchester carrying banners, in a law-abiding, good-natured fashion which was the despair of the political agitators, and which he found admirable. He did not say when he was coming home.

Charlotte threw down his panegyric in disgust and rode off to see Gerard.

That very afternoon Kit drove into the forecourt at Hartwood and asked for her ladyship.

Shortly after posting his letter, he had

himself heard from Edward, now back in London and worried about their grandmother, the Dowager Marchioness. He did not think there was any immediate danger but Grandmama was undoubtedly failing and he thought Kit ought to know.

Kit wrote back that he would travel south at a reasonable speed, breaking his journey at Hartwood so that he could collect Charlotte and bring her on to London with him next day.

He was not surprised to be told that she was out riding. He went up to her dressing-room, perhaps to feel the pleasure of being surrounded by her belongings, the book she was reading, and her work-table, open with the needle-cases, scissors and ivory spools all laid out in their little trays. There was a piece of paper screwed up on the carpet; he picked it up and saw that it was his last letter. Looking round for somewhere to put it, he lifted the flap of her secretaire and found another letter lying just inside.

Kit was not the sort of man who spied on his wife or even expected to be shown her correspondence. It was a glance of casual, unsuspecting innocence that was riveted by the words, in Gerard's well-known hand:

'*My adored Charlotte . . .*'

An hour later Charlotte arrived home, to

be greeted by the news that Kit had returned. She hurried joyfully indoors. All her grievances had vanished (which just showed what a good thing it was to have one's own amusements, instead of sitting at home and brooding). In the hall she met the groom of the chambers.

'Where is his lordship, Hobson?'

'I believe I heard him go into the library, my lady.'

Charlotte almost ran into the library. Kit was standing in front of the high window, she saw him only as a dark silhouette. Casting down her riding-whip and gloves, she went towards him, smiling.

'What a charming surprise! I'm sorry I was out—'

'With your lover, I assume? You adulterous trollop!'

Her heart lurched and she gasped as though she had been winded.

'How did you—who said I was—'

'I should have known what would happen! You've been living in his pocket for the last year, I might have guessed that you were betraying me all the while—'

'I wasn't, Kit! It was never like that.'

'Don't lie to me!'

He crossed the room and seized her by the shoulders. For a moment she thought he was going to strangle her, then he flung her backwards so violently that she almost fell. His eyes had turned the colour of steel, they were hostile and contemptuous. The hands that had gripped her so unmercifully had bruised her to the bone.

Charlotte was very frightened but she was a fighter; she was not going to be bullied into accepting the accusation that she had been deceiving him for several months. Her attempts to explain sounded self-justifying rather than penitent, which was a mistake. At last he seemed to understand, though if he believed her this did nothing to placate him.

'Am I to congratulate you?' he enquired sarcastically, 'on remaining faithful to me for so long? Nearly three years! I suppose I must count myself lucky.'

'Well, you have very little cause to complain,' retorted Charlotte, rubbing her elbow, which she had knocked on the corner of one of the bookcases when he pushed her. 'If you had not gone off and left me alone this would never have happened.'

'So it's my fault, is it, that you're a whore? And a damned impudent whore into the bargain.'

'I'm not a—I'm not what you said! You've no reason to call me such a disgusting name.' She was genuinely outraged, for she had never heard anyone use the word before (except when reading from the Bible or acting Shakespeare). 'I've done nothing worse than plenty of our friends. Olivia, for instance. You don't use such horrible language about her.'

'That's entirely different.'

'Yes, it would be. She was your mistress and I'm only your wife.'

The door opened a fraction and Hobson appeared respectfully in the gap.

Kit said, 'Get out.'

Hobson stood his ground. 'I beg your pardon, my lord, I think I should inform you that an express has arrived from Lord Edward—'

'Oh. Very well, I'll come.'

As he left the library, Kit removed the key from the door, and then Charlotte heard the lock turn on the outer side. She was a prisoner. He had locked her in.

She rushed over to the door, frantically twisting the handle, banging on the panels and shouting.

'Let me out! Let me out!'

No one took any notice.

Charlotte had a horror of being locked up, ever since a cruel nursemaid had once shut her in a dark cupboard. She collapsed on to the sofa too stunned to think clearly.

Presently Kit came back. He spoke to her in a hard impersonal voice.

'I shall have to leave for London immediately. My grandmother is asking for me, and they say she will not live above a day or two. Everything else will have to wait. But of course you realize, Charlotte, that I shall not be taking you to Scotland, nor anywhere else, for a long time to come. You have had enough spoiling and indulgence to ruin you for life, and it's time I taught you to behave yourself.'

'How do you mean to do that?' asked Charlotte, cowed yet still faintly rebellious.

Kit picked up the whip she had thrown down when she came in, and swung it lightly in his hand.

'If necessary I shall beat you,' he said dispassionately.

She stared at him, all the defiance shocked out of her.

He laid down the whip. His expression was grim.

'One more thing before I go. I haven't time to see Winton—my grandmother must come first. In the meanwhile you are not to see him or write to him. Is that clear? I've been too soft with you in the past, but I warn you, it will be different from now on.'

Ten minutes later he left for London.

Charlotte was still in the library, wrestling with the effects of fear, resentment and pure temper. Guilt too, though in a lesser degree. She supposed that what she had done was wrong—very well then: she *knew* it was wrong according to the strict Christian principles she had been taught as a girl. But surely these rules were a counsel of perfection, hardly anyone succeeded in keeping them, and she had at least felt some compunction about making Kit unhappy; it was the one thing which would have brought her a real sense of guilt, she had been dimly aware of this all along. Only Kit was not unhappy, he was a domineering tyrant who thought of nothing but his rights, including the right to subdue her by force. His furious anger had relieved her conscience. He had acted like a brute, abused and misjudged her, called her a vile name, locked her up and threatened to beat her. In the world they belonged to she thought that such behaviour would be far more severely condemned than a discreet love affair between two persons of equal birth.

This reminded her of Gerard. What was she to do about him? She felt an obligation to warn him, whatever Kit might threaten. In any case, if she drove herself over to Troughton without taking a groom, no one would know where she had been. The idea of something definite to do made her feel better; she pulled the bellrope.

When the footman answered, she asked for her phaeton to be got ready.

'Before dinner, my lady?' asked the man, surprised.

'Tell them to put off dinner,' said Charlotte who had lost all sense of time.

The man bowed and withdrew. Shortly afterwards Hobson appeared, saying he deeply regretted that there was something amiss with the shaft of the phaeton.

'Is there? It was perfectly all right yesterday. Tell them to send round one of the other carriages then. A gig that I can drive myself.'

'It's rather late, my lady.'

'Well, what of it? The men can hardly complain of being overworked.'

Hobson, acutely ill-at-ease, murmured something about his lordship's orders. Then she understood. Kit had left instructions that she was not to use any of the horses or carriages while he was away. She did not question the wretched Hobson, it would serve no purpose beyond embarrassing them both. Better to pretend she had changed her mind because it was now raining.

But it was the final humiliation, that Kit should have disgraced her in front of their servants. I'll make him sorry for this, she raged inwardly.

CHAPTER TWELVE

In the middle of the night Charlotte decided
how she was going to bring Kit to his senses.
She would leave Hartwood secretly. When he
came back he would find her gone and he
would not know where to look for her. He
would be filled with remorse and alarm, he
would also find it very awkward to explain
her absence. And serve him right, thought
Charlotte, whose resentment had now
reached a point where she really thought she
was the injured party.

The fact was that she had been far more
frightened by Kit's anger than she could bear
to admit, even to herself. The Rivers girls
had not endured the harsh upbringing that
was thought right in so many homes. Lady
Rivers believed in gentler measures, she
would not allow her daughters to be slapped,
much less whipped. The only tyrant in their
nursery—the woman who locked Charlotte in
a cupboard—had been dismissed the following day. To Charlotte the idea that she could
be locked up or beaten seemed absolutely
barbarous. Since she was naturally coura-
geous, she would not have cared to run away
because she was afraid, so it was providential

that she had hit on such an excellent reason for leaving Hartwood.

Only the question was, where could she go? Her first idea, a flight to her parents' house in Surrey, was quite unpractical. It was the first place Kit would look for her, and though they would undoubtedly be on her side, Charlotte could not help feeling that Papa and Mama would want her to go back to Kit directly he asked for her. A wife who left her husband's roof and refused to return was committing social suicide, and Charlotte had no intention of doing that. What she needed was to stay well hidden somewhere, so that Kit could not tell her to come home. She would write to him, giving no address, and he could place an advertisement in the *Morning Post* when he was properly chastened and ready to meet on her terms. All she needed was a safe refuge.

And then she thought of West Park.

The Rendals had been planning a tour of Switzerland this summer, Charlotte had supposed them already across the Channel when she heard from Sally: there had been some complication (due to Rupert Rendal's money troubles probably) and they were high and dry at West Park. This news had come while Kit was in Manchester. He would never suspect that Charlotte was with the

Rendals, since he imagined they were on the Continent. She would go there tomorrow. She would have to travel post, and there was one remaining difficulty—she hadn't enough money to get her to Berkshire.

She still had to warn Gerard that Kit had discovered their affair and she felt sure he would lend her the money.

Next morning she put her plan into operation. It was rather difficult to equip herself for a journey without confiding in Turnbull, who had charge of all her clothes, but Charlotte had one piece of luck; her luggage had been fetched from some distant part of the house in preparation for the Scottish trip. She seized on the smallest portmanteau, collected a few necessities, and made a cautious escape from the house. When she came to the edge of the forest she turned and looked back at the beautiful rose-red building where she had been so ecstatically happy, and experienced a moment of panic. What was she doing, running away from home? She must be out of her mind. If her precious little Will had been at Hartwood she could not have dragged herself a step further. But Will was not there and Kit had become a tyranical stranger who hated and ill-treated her. Doggedly she started on her three mile walk to Troughton.

It was not raining, which was a blessing,

and she was a good walker. If only the warm, damp weather had not been so oppressive, and the portmanteau such a nuisance to carry.

At last she arrived at Troughton House. Gerard was startled by her appearance and led her into the deserted drawing-room.

'What's happened, Char? What's the matter?'

He grew more and more horrified as she poured out her story. He was very shaken to hear that Kit had found them out, but soon his only concern was for Charlotte and the way Kit had treated her.

'I'd like to break his neck!'

This reminded her of something else that was worrying her. 'You won't fight him, will you? Promise me.'

'My dear, I shall have to, if he calls me out.'

'Perhaps he won't. He doesn't approve of duelling.'

'It seems he doesn't approve of adultery either,' said Gerard. 'In spite of having been such a famous practitioner himself.'

They stood silent, lost in thought. She was seeing him quite differently today, all the charms of dalliance had been quenched and her senses felt completely numb. Still, she was more than ever glad of Gerard's kindness and devotion.

'Kit used to have a shocking temper as a boy,' he was saying. 'I thought he had learnt to master it by now. I suppose he can't help being jealous.'

'That's no excuse,' said Charlotte, who had grown up thinking jealousy the worst of the vices. (Little Charlotte is never jealous.) And how right she had been, when the sickening disease had such an ugly effect. 'A jealous man wants to possess people as though they were chattels. When he locked me in the library, it was like the butler locking up the silver . . . Will you do something for me, Gerard?'

'Anything in the world,' he declared, casting a rather apprehensive glance at the portmanteau which she had brought into the drawing-room and dumped on his mother's polished rosewood table. She told him what she planned to do, and asked if he would lend her the money for the post-chaise. She had been half afraid that he would try to discourage her, but Gerard was so anxious to get her safely out of Kit's reach that he actually volunteered to escort her to West Park.

'You need not put yourself to the trouble. It is hardly more than half a day's journey.'

'You've never travelled anywhere without your own carriage and servants, you would

129

find it very awkward. Of course I shall accompany you.'

The Wintons did not keep a private travelling-chariot, so a servant was sent to the Colbrook Arms in Troughton to order a chaise-and-four.

They neither of them enjoyed the drive to Berkshire. A shutter of private reservations had closed between them. Gerard wore a hangdog expression, as though he felt he was chiefly to blame for the whole disaster. The wet summer had cast a blight on the country-side, everywhere they saw fields of rugged corn flattened in sodden rows, unripe fruit on the trees, dejected villagers.

Charlotte was thankful when they turned into the gateway of West Park. She and Gerard held a hasty conference.

'Would you like me to go in first and talk to the Rendals?' he asked.

'Thank you, but I had better see Sally myself. Alone, I think, if you don't mind.'

Sally was delighted to see her; she was bored to death and a visit from dearest Charlotte was providential. The news that dearest Charlotte was in the throes of a dramatic affair with Gerard Winton made her crow with triumph and say, 'I knew you would fall into his arms sooner or later.'

Her expression altered when she heard of

Kit's uncompromising anger, and when she realized that Charlotte was hoping to take refuge at West Park she was frankly appalled.

'It's quite impossible—you must be mad to think of such a thing.'

'I am very sorry if it is inconvenient—have you other guests? I never thought of that.'

No, they were quite alone. Sally's objections were based on something entirely different, she seemed to be having an unusual fit of morality.

'Rupert and I cannot lend support to a wife who is running away from her husband. I wonder you should ask it of us.'

'I'm not running away! I merely want to keep out of sight for a short while, so that I can't be forced into doing anything so definite. Gerard seemed to think it was a good idea.'

'Oh, did he? I had better talk to Master Gerard.'

Sally rang the bell and told the servant to show in Mr Winton, and to fetch Mr Rendal as well. She moved restlessly about her drawing-room while they waited, talking affectedly and pretending this was an ordinary social call. Charlotte watched her in a state of dumb astonishment.

As soon as Gerard had joined them, Sally began to reproach him for placing her in such an awkward situation, calling on her husband to back her up, which was rather hard on him, as he hardly knew what they were talking about. When it was made clear to him, he looked extremely concerned.

'I wish it was in our power to help you, Lady Brancaster. Unhappily it is out of the question.'

'I cannot see why,' said Gerard, glancing from Rendal to Sally. 'Charlotte has stayed in your house before without her husband. That is all she wants to do now. You need not become any further involved in our difficulties—we are not asking you to condone a public scandal. There has been no scandal and there will be none. I hoped I might leave Charlotte in your care but I had no intention of cadging an invitation for myself.'

Charlotte remembered with a sort of dull wonder that last year she and Gerard had been deliberately invited here to meet each other and put into adjoining rooms. What was happening now seemed quite incomprehensible.

'That's all very well,' replied Sally, 'but we cannot be expected to risk offending people who have the disposal of so much patronage.'

And gradually it came out that Rupert was hoping for a minor court appointment, a well-paid sinecure which would help to restore their finances. Mr Chance had promised to speak to Lord Liverpool. If Brancaster found out that the Rendals were encouraging his wife to defy him, he could ruin their prospects.

'He would never do such a thing!' protested Charlotte, surprised into defending Kit. 'He's not spiteful.'

'According to you, he's beside himself with jealousy,' Sally pointed out. 'And we have too much at stake. I know Lord Brancaster does not always support the Ministry; all the same he's a great Tory lord, and no one who holds office at present will favour those who have displeased him.'

Charlotte stood up. 'We'll leave at once.'

'It's getting late,' said Rupert, perhaps a little ashamed of his wife. 'If you were to stay the night—'

'No, thank you, I won't trespass on your charity.'

As they were being shown out, Gerard turned to Sally and said in his most agreeable manner, 'If you toady hard enough, I dare say Brancaster will offer Rendal my seat in the House of Commons. He will be looking for a new member.'

Charlotte swept proudly out of the house, her head held high, but once they were in the

133

carriage and the front door closed behind them, she could not mask her distress.

'I thought she was my friend.'

'A fair-weather friend if ever there was one.'

'Oh, Gerard, I'm so thankful you are not like that.'

They had been uneasy and distant with each other during the drive; now she turned to him spontaneously and they were tenderly embracing when one of the postboys came round to the side of the chaise and tapped on the window, asking for directions. Where did they want to go?

'Good heavens, I have no idea.' Gerard was thrown out of his stride. He released Charlotte and did his best to sound convincingly respectable. 'We have had to change our plans. Bad news. My—my wife is rather upset. You had better take us to a comfortable inn.'

'Very good, sir,' said the man, grinning.

They jolted off (neither of them noticing the shrubbery where they had walked last autumn) and Gerard said, 'I ought to have pretended you were my sister.'

Charlotte had a hysterical desire to giggle. 'Rather an incestuous kind of sister—I don't think that would have added much to our consequence.'

134

'Perhaps not.' He took her hand, smiling. 'The thing is I am afraid we shall have to go on posing as a married couple at this inn. The post-boys will get their supper in the kitchen, while their horses are resting, and I dare say they will report on our strange goings-on. If we tell the people there a different story we shall be simply courting notoriety.'

Charlotte shrugged. 'It can't be helped. What shall we call ourselves?'

Gerard suggested Smith.

'Not very distinguished!'

'Come, there is Sidney Smith, the hero of Acre.'

'And the other Sydney Smith, the wit.'

'Not to speak of our old friend Adam Smith.'

As he mentioned that contentious name, she felt a pang of almost physical pain because it called up so many memories she could not bear at present. But they were pulling up at an inn and she went inside quite cheerfully on his arm. The Rendals' rebuff had drawn them closer together.

The Hare and Hounds was a posting-house on the Bath Road, standing on its own at a convenient place for travellers to change horses. There were no other visitors actually staying in the house and Gerard was able to engage the only private parlour, so they felt

135

fairly secure.

Over supper they discussed what Charlotte was to do next.

'I really think your wisest course,' said Gerard, 'would be to go to your parents. I can escort you to Surrey tomorrow, and there is no reason why Brancaster should ever be told that we did not go there direct from Hartwood. And Lord Rivers will be able to protect you better than anyone.'

Charlotte was now ready to agree. Stunned by the first shock of Kit's anger, her one instinct had been to reach a place where he could not possibly find her. That was only twenty-four hours ago, but she had just passed the longest and most wearisome day of her life, the scene in the library at Hartwood was a little dimmed, and if he did come to look for her at Clutton her father would be bound to take her part and act as a mediator.

She ate a little boiled capon, drank the two glasses of claret that Gerard pressed on her, and then went to bed, completely worn out. Because she was still so young her exhaustion sent her to sleep in spite of all her anxieties. During those amorous afternoons at Troughton Gerard had several times said he wished they could spend a whole night together. Now he had his wish, and much good it did him. Charlotte lay like the dead, unaware of him lying tense and miserable beside her, of bars of light sloping across their window as people with lanterns moved about in the yard below, of some late arrivals being shown to a room further along the passage.

As Charlotte and Gerard went down to breakfast next morning, the landlord was lying in wait for them in the hall. He greeted them with an effusiveness that was slightly defensive.

'I trust you slept well, madam. And you too, sir. We have a little sun at last, you perceive. I hope it will not be disagreeable to you, sir: I have arranged for another lady and gentleman to breakfast with you in the private parlour. They have been staying at Longleat and came in late last night, having been delayed on the road. I explained that you had engaged the parlour, but I said to them, "I am sure Mr and Mrs Smith will understand."'

It was clear that the people who had been staying at Longleat cut a great deal more ice with the landlord than a Mr and Mrs Smith. Gerard was annoyed and began to protest. The thought flashed into Charlotte's mind that she was probably acquainted with a good many of the people who stayed at Longleat. But the parlour door was ajar, the landlord

137

had somehow got behind her, urging her in, and she was obliged to walk forward and confront the couple who were already seated at the breakfast table.

'Why, Cousin Charlotte!' exclaimed Virgilia Danby. 'And Mr Winton!'

Charlotte turned, pushing past the inn-keeper, and fled upstairs.

CHAPTER THIRTEEN

'I suppose there is no hope of persuading them to keep quiet?' asked Charlotte, 'to pretend they didn't see us?'

'No hope at all,' said Gerard gloomily. 'He means to circulate the story through every London club with the greatest relish, and she will do the same in all the best drawing-rooms.'

Charlotte was sitting on the unmade bed. There was a cup of tepid coffee on the night-table but she could not swallow it.

'Perhaps if I was to talk to Virgilia—'

'No,' he said decisively. 'I beg you won't attempt to do anything of the sort. It's no use throwing yourself on the mercy of people like the Danbys. I have found that already. You must remember that he has disliked us in-tensely ever since you rejected him at West Park and I sent him packing. Naturally he won't have given his wife the correct version of that episode, but he has told her something and they are both equally hostile.'

'It was such infernally back luck meeting them.'

'We should never have put up at a posting-inn on the Bath Road, there was always a danger of running into someone we knew. It's my fault, I ought to have known better.'

Charlotte was inclined to agree, so she said nothing, rather pointedly.

Then it struck her that this disaster need not have happened if she had accepted Rupert Rendal's grudging invitation and spent the night at West Park before travelling on to Surrey. She had been too proud to accept favours from the Rendals—without realizing that pride was a luxury she could not afford. As a result she had broken the unwritten law and put herself in the wrong by every standard. Her original affair with Gerard had been absolutely discreet; she had not behaved well but she honestly believed that Kit had behaved worse. Once she had been caught staying with her lover at a public inn, using an assumed name, there was no doubt whatever that Kit had the right to be as angry as he chose. He could turn her out of doors and nobody in society would receive her.

'What am I to do?' she asked in a frightened voice.

Gerard was moving about the room. He was somewhere behind her, out of her line of vision, when he said, 'I think there's only one thing we can do. We must go abroad.'

She spun round, staring at him. 'Go

abroad? Together?'

'I know it's not at all the right life for you, but I can't see that we have any choice. I'm sorry, Charlotte. It's all my fault—'

'Please stop saying everything is your fault. I brought this on myself. And there is an alternative—I must go to my parents, as we planned. They won't turn me away.'

'No, of course not. That is to say, they will be willing to help you, I am sure, and make any necessary arrangements about money and so on. But you do realize, Charlotte, that you cannot hope to live with Lord and Lady Rivers and mix in society once you have been the subject of a scandal? It would be an impossible position for them and for your sisters.'

This was a most unwelcome idea but he was probably right. Females who got into serious scrapes were generally relegated to some obscure backwater where they could not cause embarrassment.

'Of course I'll marry you,' he said. 'You know that, don't you? If and when you are free to marry again.'

'You mean, if Kit divorces me? Do you think he will?' She knew next to nothing about divorce.

'He'd have to bring an action for crim. con. and then get a private bill through Parliament. It wouldn't be difficult.'

Criminal conversation was the rather absurd euphemism for what had passed between her and Gerard that afternoon in the forest, and in his room at Troughton House. Although she now admitted to herself that she had been silly and irresponsible, she still could not feel she was a criminal. In theory she had given to Gerard something which belonged to Kit, only it had not been at all like that: she had made love with Gerard when Kit was not there (actually because Kit was not there) but this had not lessened by one iota the much greater intensity of passionate love which she would have given Kit on his return. Perhaps if she could explain properly he might still forgive her. Only it was too late, she had created the sort of scandal which no husband would ignore.

Gerard was saying something important that she must listen to.

'There is sometimes a clause inserted in a divorce bill to prevent the wife making a second marriage. As a sop to please the moralists.'

Charlotte did not care whether she would be able to marry again or not. A divorced woman was such a complete outcast, they would never let her see her baby. Then it dawned on her that she had probably lost him

142

already. Leaning her head on her arms, she began to weep.

Gerard, hovering anxiously above her, had the sense to realize she would rather be alone. He tiptoed away, like someone leaving a sick room.

Presently a housemaid with a broom looked in at the door.

'Please go away,' said Charlotte.

The girl went, but not before she had taken a long, inquisitive stare. As though she had never seen an adulteress before, thought Charlotte savagely.

Gerard came back and said the sooner they cleared out of this pot-house the better. The landlord was making himself most unpleasant.

'Where are we to go?'

'I suggest we should hire a chaise and remove to some quiet inn well away from the busy post-roads—somewhere we can stay in peace for a few days while you think over my proposal.'

So that was what they did. They discovered a village called Bagston where they felt sure they had no aquaintance. The Holly Bush Inn was clean but unpretentious; they took the only bedroom and arranged for sole possession of a coffee room which smelt as though no one had used it for a year. Here they dragged out the rest of an unreal and depressing day. That night Gerard tried to liberate Charlotte's emotions by making love to her, which was not a great success.

She was very sorry for him. Swamped by her own desperate unhappiness, she had the grace to recognize his loyalty. She was *ruined* but he was not. Apart from the risk of having to fight a duel (and duelling was very much frowned on these days) he would not be banished from the great world for his part in the scandal. Yet he had offered without a moment's hesitation to go and live abroad with her, promising to marry her if he could. True, he was in love with her, but that cut both ways, for he must have guessed by now that she was not in love with him. In her gratitude she felt she must do everything to avoid hurting him.

Armed with good intentions, she agreed to take a turn in the fresh air next morning. They followed a footpath across a field and paused, leaning over a gate, to gaze at the long, straight line of a canal which ran across the quiet green landscape. Some way off, moving very slowly, they could see a man with a horse on the towpath, pulling a loaded boat.

Gerard began to discuss their future on the Continent, speaking as though it was already a settled thing.

I thought one of the German states, perhaps. There are many charming little spas where one can have some pleasant company without the fuss and regimentation of a court.' Which, being interpreted, meant that the divorced wife of an English marquess might be accepted in an easy-going society that was constantly changing. 'German music is always very good, which you would like, and we might buy a property and amuse ourselves improving it. We should be in the heart of the Gothic country you know, and that would give us endless opportunities!'

'How kind you are,' she said impulsively. 'Ready to abandon so much for my sake. Your political career—'

'I don't regard it, I assure you. Besides which I could not hope to retain the Troughton seat, in the circumstances.'

'You might be offered another. And what about your mother? She would miss you dreadfully if you were to live permanently abroad.'

'Yes, I do feel rather concerned about her,' he admitted. 'Would you object if I was to come over occasionally to visit her?'

'Of course not,' said Charlotte, to whom this was all a kind of make-believe. Anxious to please him, she continued the fantasy. 'I don't suppose your mother would care to travel so far at her age, but perhaps Letty would come and stay with us in our Gothic castle.'

Gerard frowned. 'That would hardly do.'

'If we were married,' Charlotte said hastily. 'I would not expect her to approve the present situation, but if I became your wife, I assume your sister would be able to meet me?'

'I should not ask it of her. But we have more urgent matters to consider—'

'Wait a moment, Gerard: I want to know why you would not ask Letty to meet me. Do you think I might lead her astray?'

As Letty Winton was a rather dowdy spinster of thirty-six, this was not very kind.

'Surely I don't have to explain. You must know I cannot expect my mother and sister to meet you, after what has happened.'

His fair, handsome face wore a solemn look; it was not at all the expression with which Kit had called her an impudent whore, but it gave her the same sensation of hot, burning resentment in the pits of her stomach.

'After *what* has happened?' she exploded. 'Do you mean my becoming your mistress or our being discovered together by the Danbys? Suppose Kit had never read your letter, suppose we had all continued as we were before—would you have encouraged Letty to visit me at Hartwood next winter?'

'That would have been different. So long as she did not know—'

'Well, of all the blatant pieces of hypocrisy I ever heard! Oh, I know that is how things are managed in the world at large. It would be too awkward to have society split into warring factions by every divorce, so people all side with propriety and the injured husband. I dare say they are right. But inside our own families, it seems quite monstrous. Am I no longer fit to associate with your sister, even privately? Are you ashamed of me?'

'No, no! Of course not—my dear Char, how could you imagine anything so horrible?'

Even while he protested too much, his glance slid uneasily away from her and she saw that he was ashamed—of having a mistress who had been found out, who had fallen from her natural place, a disreputable person to be shunned and despised by other women. He loved her still and certainly desired her (for how long?) But his offers of protection and marriage had been made because he felt responsible for her plight and his chief emotion was probably pity.

The man with his horse on the towpath was

level with them now and plodding patiently by, the boat gliding after them through the water. Charlotte drew a deep breath.

'As you say, it's pointless to argue. Shall we go on a little further?'

She was very silent during the rest of their walk, and when they got back to the Holly Bush she complained of a racking headache.

Gerard asked what he could do for her. Charlotte, who had counted on this, said she would give anything for some laudanum drops. Gerard hired a horse and set off to look for an apothecary in the nearby market town. As soon as he had gone, she got up from the bed where she was supposed to be prostrated and opened the drawer where Gerard had stowed his spare money. She borrowed five sovereigns, scribbled him a few lines of gratitude and farewell, and stuffed her bedraggled possessions into the portmanteau. She left the inn without meeting a soul in the torpor of early afternoon, walked to the livery stable she had noticed at the other end of the village, and engaged a carriage to take her on the first stage of her journey.

This time she was running away from Gerard.

CHAPTER FOURTEEN

Charlotte had never wanted to leave Kit permanently nor to elope with Gerard to the Continent. For just one day, shattered by their encounter with the Danbys, she had half believed that these drastic steps were being forced on her. Gerard had implied this, but mercifully she had seen through Gerard in time: a priggish libertine, disapproving of the woman he had seduced without being villain enough to abandon her. How could I have made a fool of myself with such a poor creature, she thought in disgust. And a man who worried so much about propriety was not likely to be the best judge of her situation. Surely there was still some hope of saving her marriage?

She dared not face Kit directly on his own ground by going straight to Brancaster House or back to Hartwood, and her first plan, when she decided to slip away from the Holly Bush, had been to go to her parents' country estate, a refuge she had considered all along. Then she had remembered that the house would be full of visitors, including Sir Augustus and Lady Palmer and their son, the young man who was in love with Mary. It would be dreadfully awkward if Charlotte were to arrive in a post-chaise, alone, unheralded and looking as though she had been dragged through a hedge backwards (which was how she felt she looked after two days without Turnbull). She did not want to spoil Mary's time of special happiness, and she had then thought of a sensible alternative. Although her father's house in Berkeley Street was nominally shut up for the summer, there were always a few servants there and a bed available for any of the family who needed to spend a night in town. She had decided to instal herself in Berkeley Street, writing to Kit from there, and also to her father for she would be glad of his support.

She was stiff and weary by the time her chaise turned off Piccadilly into Berkeley Street, which was beginning to have a deserted air, many of the brass knockers had been taken off the doors, a sign that their owners had already left London. Her father's house was officially closed, though Charlotte was surprised to see a carriage and four drawn up outside and then to recognize, as it moved off, that it was her parents' carriage with the crest on the door and their old coachman in the Rivers livery. Someone had just arrived: she wondered who it was and why.

One of the post-boys took out her port-manteau and rapped on the door with the flat of his hand. She paid him and stood waiting on the doorstep, feeling flustered and apprehensive.

The door was opened a fraction by a shirt-sleeved minion she did not know, and she heard her father say urgently from inside the hall, 'We are not at home to callers.'

The door was nearly slammed in her face, and she called out, 'Tell him to let me in, Papa! It's me—Charlotte!'

Lord Rivers wrenched open the door, seized her by the arm and pulled her into the house.

'Charlotte—thank God we've found you! Is that scoundrel with you?'

'What scoundrel? Oh, you mean Gerard. No, I left him in a village that I've forgotten the name of.'

'Well, never mind that now, come upstairs,' said Lord Rivers hurrying her past the servant who had very large red ears. 'Your mother is in the drawing-room.'

The drawing-room was under dust sheets. Lady Rivers, looking fragile and distracted, was sitting on one of the swaddled sofas. When she saw her daughter, she gave a cry that was almost a moan.

'My poor, misguided child, how could you

do anything so dreadful? How could you leave your husband and child to run off with Mr Winton?'

'I didn't run off with him, Mama—it was all a stupid mistake. But what have you heard?'

Though it was a relief to have her parents here on the spot, she was rather alarmed to find that the report of her indiscretion had spread so quickly. She was now informed that the Danbys had gone straight to Kit, which was something she might have expected; Virgilia was always so proud of being related to the Colbrooks. Kit's anger had been so intense that Edward had been frightened of what he might do and had ridden down to Surrey to consult Lord and Lady Rivers. They had come up to town, leaving Amelia to act as hostess to their house-party with a vague, face-saving excuse that Charlotte was seriously ill.

While she was trying to disentangle these facts her parents were trying to discover the truth about her elopement—for of course it had sounded like an elopement to them. When Charlotte tried to explain they became understandably confused.

'But if you were not running away, what was Kit so angry about? It sounds quite unlike him to become violently jealous without the smallest provocation.'

'Well, he did have some provocation, Mama.'

'Just what were you doing, Charlotte?' asked her father.

'Going to bed with Gerard Winton,' said Charlotte brazenly, to hide her dislike of having to make the admission.

She saw her mother flinch at this frankness.

Her father said, 'Don't you think Brancaster had some right to be angry?'

'But he was quite unreasonable. He locked me in the library and said he would beat me!'

'Ten to one he never meant it. He is far too great a gentleman,' said Lady Rivers, who seemed to have some romantic misconceptions about her son-in-law. 'But why did you behave so improperly? Surely you are not in love with Winton?'

'My dear Aimée,' said Lord Rivers, 'we had better accept the fact that Charlotte was unfaithful to Brancaster because he wouldn't take her to Scotland on the day she wanted to go. That's pretty near the truth, isn't it?' he challenged his daughter.

'I suppose so, Papa,' muttered Charlotte sulkily. Put like that it did sound quite shocking.

'And for a fit of pique,' he added, 'you

153

have dishonoured your husband's name and caused a public scandal.'

'But need there be a scandal? I have been thinking. If the Danbys went straight to Kit, he had it in his power to prevent them from gossiping about me. Virgilia would do anything to please Cousin Brancaster.'

'Edward tells me that Kit lost his temper with Danby and ordered him out of the house. Edward was surprised, after that, at his brother's paying so much attention to the malice of a man he despised. Of course I realize now that he had grounds for believing that the story was true.'

Lady Rivers pressed her handkerchief to her eyes. Surrounded by the shrouded ghosts of her drawing-room furniture in their holland covers, she had sunk into a mood of plaintive reproach.

'I wonder if you understand the harm you have wrought on us? We shall all be made to suffer, Papa and I and your poor little boy. Amelia and Mary too—who is going to marry them once their sister's disgrace becomes known? Fulton and Giles Palmer will cry

'Oh come, Mama—that is quite absurd!' said Charlotte uncomfortably. She glanced at her father who was usually so good at coping with Mama's nerves, but he looked grave and said nothing.

'I don't know how you could be so foolish and wicked, so lost to everything you have been taught! Brought up so carefully and married to a good and devoted husband, I can't think how you became so depraved,' Lady Rivers complained.

This was too much.

'I copied you,' said Charlotte bluntly. 'Not in causing a scandal. I know I was a perfect fool to go travelling about in Gerard's company and let myself be seen. But all my troubles started because I had done with him what you have been doing with Lord St Eudo ever since I can remember.'

She saw her mother's mouth open, a blind, dark, tragic look came into her eyes. The beautiful face seemed to crumble.

'Hold your tongue, you spiteful hussy!' exclaimed Lord Rivers. 'Haven't you done enough harm already? Leave the room immediately!'

'Yes, Papa,' said Charlotte, abashed into the obedience of childhood.

She heard her mother say, in a voice of anguish, 'I never thought my own child would cast such a stone.'

'My dearest Aimée, don't distress yourself; she did not know what she was saying.'

'Oh yes, she did, and she was right. I have been a wicked woman and now I am being punished for it.'

Charlotte slipped out of the room.

She went and sat on the stairs that ran up through the narrow London house to the bedrooms above. Her legs would not carry her any further. So many people in the last few days—Kit, the Rendals, Gerard and now her parents—had taken such an unexpectedly black view of what she had done that she was beginning to wonder whether she had misunderstood the rules that governed society. Of course nobody said openly what they did or felt; they spoke in the language of pious morality, or in the language of sensibility which was equally baffling. Was it possible that half the recognized lovers in their circle were merely indulging in long-standing flirtations? Not that it made much difference now. To have ruined her marriage for such a trivial adventure was certainly indefensible, like risking your neck to steal an apple when you were not even hungry. She had simply thought she could eat the apple without falling out of the tree.

Lord Rivers emerged from the drawing-room. He said coldly, 'I hope you will never speak to your mother in that way again. Her nerves are not equal to supporting such deliberate unkindness.'

Charlotte noted that her mother could pick

all the apples she wanted without paying for them. It seemed very unfair but she made no comment. She had never heard her father speak in that distant voice before. She was his favourite child, his namesake—she was Charlotte because he was Charles—and he had been so proud of the fearless, active girl who had partly consoled him for not having a son.

His expression softened a little. 'You are very young still, and all may not be lost. I shall go round to Brancaster House and tell Kit you are here. Do you think you had better write him a note?'

'Oh yes, I must certainly do so.'

'Don't try to justify yourself. You will have to be humble, Char.'

Humility was not Charlotte's strong suit, but it came easily to her this evening, for the events of the past four days had undermined her self-esteem. She explained why she had been with Gerard at the Hare and Hounds, adding: *I do not write this to excuse my conduct, for I know that no excuse is possible. I am deeply sensible of the wrong I have done. I simply want to remove the suspicion that I was running away with Gerard. I have never wished to be anything except your wife and I can only beg you to forgive me and take me back. If you do, I promise that I will never again give you the slightest cause to distrust me, or to regret your generosity*.

It sounded dreadfully artificial, not at all the way she and Kit really talked to each other. That was the worst of a letter. She impressed on her father all the details of her plan for going to Berkshire, hoping he would be able to convince Kit that she had been reckless and stupid but nothing worse.

It was no good. When Lord Rivers returned two hours later, he had to report a complete failure. Though Kit had listened in silence to all his father-in-law had to say, he had refused to meet Charlotte or even to read her letter. He wanted nothing more to do with her. He would spare her the humiliation of being divorced, but that was his only concession. They were to live apart, on terms that he would dictate.

It was a crushing blow. Up to that moment, in spite of all her fears, all the planning and play-acting with Gerard, she had nursed a secret belief that Kit would take her back. They had loved each other so much. If only she could see him . . .

'I'll go round there myself,' she said, white-faced and desperate.

'I'm afraid you won't get into the house. He's told the porter you are not to be let in.'

Charlotte remembered that he had told the servants at Hartwood she was not to have horses or carriages. He was not only implacable but thorough.

'Then I'll go and lie in the road outside,' she threatened hysterically. 'And he'll have to drive over me.'

Her father looked at her with a mixture of pity and irritation.

'You won't make him change his mind by behaving like Caroline Lamb.'

All the same Charlotte was determined to make a personal appeal to Kit if she could. She slipped out next morning before breakfast and walked across the Park. There was no risk of being seen by anyone she knew, so early in the day and in August at that. At Brancaster House she was met by an angel with a flaming sword in the shape of Hankey the porter, a very shaken and bemused old angel, for he had always been her devoted slave and could hardly bear to refuse her admission to her own home.

'I don't know what to do for the best, my lady. I dursen't disobey his lordship, but then it don't seem right—suppose I was to fetch Lord Edward to speak to your ladyship?'

'Yes, do fetch him for me, Hankey. I'll wait.'

She withdrew into a little room on the right of the hall, where slightly ungenteel persons

159

were put when no one knew what to do with them. Clearly she had now fallen into this category herself. She stayed there for what seemed like an age; what was Edward doing? Perhaps he would refuse to do anything for her? He must hate her now, considering how he adored Kit.

She peeped into the hall, there was no one about so she tiptoed across to the morning-room, where she managed very quietly to open the door a crack. She caught the sound of voices inside.

'I think you should see her,' Edward was saying, 'She is still your wife, and I'm sure she must wish she could wipe out the past two weeks.'

(So she had been misjudging Edward).

'Of course she does,' said another voice, so clipped and bitter that she hardly recognized it. 'She has thrown up a life of pleasure and consequence which she very much enjoyed, and all for a man who has left her in the lurch. I could have told her Gerard would be even more frightened of social disgrace than he is of a bullet through the head. Which is why he is not worth shooting.'

Charlotte ran into the room.

'That's not how it was, believe me, Kit! I am truly sorry, if only you will let me talk to you—'

160

'My God, this is too much!'

He got up and stood behind his chair, using it as a barrier between them. He was pale and remote, not angry as she had last seen him but something worse: it seemed that he could not bear to have her near him. The steely colour was still in his eyes and he did not even look at her.

Speaking very distinctly he said, 'I hoped I had made it plain to your father that I never want to see you again. I know you have never paid attention to what anyone told you, but you will now have to begin. I'm afraid you have no choice.'

She was defeated before she could attempt to plead her cause, for she felt quite ill with mortification and it was all she could do to choke back her sobs and whisper, 'Please don't send me away.'

Someone else came into the room.

'Is Charlotte here?' It was her father, anxiously pursuing her: he must have guessed where she had gone. 'I'm sorry, Brancaster. I did try to convince her . . . Char, my dear, it will do no good to make a scene. I've come to take you home.'

The house in Berkeley Street was now the only home she had.

Next day there was a scurrilous paragraph in the *St James's Gazette* about *the young Mar-*

*chioness of Br . . . r and the enterprising member
for her husband's Borough who has been repres-
enting his lordship in a different capacity . . .*

By now even Charlotte had given up hope
of a reconciliation. Supposing Kit had agreed
to take her back, she would not be received in
society, now that her transgressions were
being publicly discussed, and he himself
might be ostracized if he condoned them.

She was plunged into a state of utter
misery. She did not know what was to
become of her and did not care.

'I wish you could remain with us, my love,'
said her mother sadly. 'Only I do not see
how—so long as your sisters are unmarried—
it is so difficult to do what is best and I am
afraid I have failed in my duty towards you
all.'

This was as near as she could get to admitting the justice of Charlotte's attack. She was
gentle and concerned while pretending that
those cruel words had never been spoken.
Fortunately Lord St Eudo was at Brighton.

One thing Aimée Rivers did do for her
daughter: she went to Brancaster House and
asked Kit if Charlotte might have Will to stay
with her sometimes. Kit refused. He was not
vindictive, he simply said that while the child
was so young constant changes and partings
might have a bad effect.

When she heard this verdict, Charlotte cried for six hours.

'My poor lamb,' said her mother, 'that must be the greatest hardship, to lose your little boy.'

'The greatest hardship,' said Charlotte bleakly, 'is to have lost the man I love.'

She meant Kit but did not trouble to say so. Lady Rivers sighed. There were times when she could not make Charlotte out.

In a material sense Kit was being generous. Charlotte was to have Pristock Manor, a good house with a fair amount of land in the West Country. It was not part of the Colbrook estate, having come into his father's hands in payment of a gaming debt. The house had been let furnished for some years and was now empty, following the death of the tenant. He was giving her the whole of her marriage settlement, which she had actually forfeited by being unfaithful.

The arrangements for her new life were drearily completed. Trunks full of her clothes, books, and other personal items came up from Hartwood, and with them came Turnbull who promptly gave notice. Lady Rivers engaged a new maid for her and persuaded Mrs Mason, her own former house-keeper, now pensioned off, to go to Pristock for the first few months and get

163

Charlotte comfortably settled in. It was also necessary to find someone who would live with her and act as her companion. After some enquiries Lady Rivers chose a Mrs Davis, a childless widow aged about thirty. Having been married, she was considered more suitable than a spinster to associate with a lady in Charlotte's unfortunate situation.

At last a day arrived when Kit and Charlotte must be present in the same room for the signing of the lengthy document which would bring their marriage virtually to an end. This solemnity took place in the Berkeley Street dining-room. Charlotte sat at one end of the mahogany table with her parents. Old Lady Brancaster had finally died, so she had gone into mourning. In her black dress she was like a wraith.

Her father's attorney was there looking prim and glum, and Mr Ferris, Kit's capable man of business whose entire time was taken up in administering the Colbrook fortune and estates. Both lawyers had clerks with them and there was a good deal of fuss, papers spread out and the placing of pens, an ink-stand and a sandbox.

The butler announced, 'Lord Brancaster and Lord Edward Colbrook.'

So now he was in the room. Charlotte found she could not look at him, though somehow she knew that he had bowed to her mother, perhaps including her in this formal gesture. A chair scraped and he sat down without speaking.

Mr Ferris began to read the Deed of Separation, which, besides including all Kit's titles, gave a list of places that Charlotte undertook not to visit: London, Brighton, Bath or the neighbourhood of Hartwood Hall in the County of Essex—anywhere she might meet the Colbrook family and their friends, or draw attention to herself. There was also a clause stating that the Marchioness would lose both house and income *if she should communicate with James Gerard Winton Esquire or ever again be guilty of a criminal association either with the said James Gerard Winton or any other person* . . .

Charlotte felt sick, staring down at her hands knotted in her lap and aware everyone in the room was trying not to look at her.

Kit said in a hard, rough voice, 'We don't want to hear all that. For God's sake, get on with it.'

'Very well, my lord.' Having to skip the rest of the paragraph, Mr Ferris became nervous. He spent some time describing a minute change he had made in the final drawing up the settlement; did Kit agree?

'Yes, certainly. So long as it is acceptable

to her ladyship.'

There was a slight pause.

'Perfectly acceptable, my lord,' said Charlotte.

She had to sign Charlotte Brancaster, rather shakily, under the single name that was his official signature. The witnesses signed as well. Then it was all over, no eleventh-hour miracle had saved her, Kit went away with Edward and she would never see him again.

Two days later she drove with Mrs Davis to Pristock Manor, the house where she was to be decently buried alive.

CHAPTER FIFTEEN

Pristock was an isolated parish on the borders of Somerset and Dorset. The village stood about two miles off the pike road. There was a church, a parsonage, an ale-house and a straggle of cottages, as well as the manor house and a fair-sized farm. All the land had been enclosed some years before and was let to the farmer, the last tenant at the Manor having wished to keep only the garden and the shooting. There was also a hamlet called Badger's Botton sunk even deeper into the landscape of inaccessible hills and valleys.

Pristock Manor itself was not quite what Charlotte was accustomed to: a gentleman's house instead of a nobleman's mansion, and an undistinguished house at that, furnished without elegance or taste. She did not care, being hardly aware of her surroundings. She was mentally stunned. The prospect before her was grim indeed. A lonely, celibate life in the depths of the country, cut off from her family, with no variety, no pleasure, nothing to look forward to. She was just twenty.

Yet that was not the worst of it. The dread of an endless grey future was still blurred by the much more acute pain of losing Kit. It was a physical agony to be without him, both as lover and friend, the strong, clever and warm-hearted man who had made her so happy and whom she had apparently destroyed, for directly he had found out about her and Gerard he had turned into a totally different person, which made her feel like a murderess. She occasionally felt sorry for Gerard (who had wisely taken himself abroad until the talk had died down) but his whole life would not be ruined by what they had done and she no longer had the slightest affection for him. She had never loved him, after all. And brooding on this, her ideas turned upside down and she saw how unnatural it was to have squandered so much on a man she cared for so little. She had clung to the excuse that such an unimportant affair could not really matter; now it seemed to her that loving should always be important, anything less was a kind of sacrilege. Perhaps she had not understood this before because hee feeling for Kit had been a young, untested love, never subjected to the strain of grief and loss. Never until now. Now, when it was too late, she was gripped by a terrible remorse.

She sat hour after hour in the dull drawing-room at Pristock Manor, looking out at the dull garden, without moving, without speaking.

Mrs Davis did her best to infuse a little life into her employer by chatting with a studied brightness and making the best of things. She was a thin, well-meaning young woman who was genuinely satisfied with her new home; life had not been easy for her since her delicate husband had died after one year of marriage. She appreciated the excellent food and thought herself well off in a spacious house with a sulky but silent young lady after some months in a cramped Bath lodging with a cantankerous old one. On their first Saturday evening she asked whether Charlotte meant to go to church next day.

'No,' said Charlotte decisively.

Mrs Davis said nothing. Charlotte guessed what she was thinking: impenitent and irreligious. In fact she was neither; she simply could not face the ordeal of being quizzed, as she imagined, by a large congregation who all knew why she had been cast off by her husband and sent here in disgrace.

'You had better take the carriage if you mean to go,' she said.

'That's very kind of you, Lady Brancaster, but I can easily walk. Half a mile each way is nothing—'

'You may as well drive. It is ridiculous to

have horses if one never uses them.'

A well-sprung chaise, a pair of carriage horses and two hacks had been sent down from Hartwood so that Charlotte could ride or drive whenever she chose. She had no desire to ride, and as for the carriage, where was she supposed to go in that? Certainly not to return calls, for none of the local gentry would call on her. Even the English love of a title could not compete with the equally English passion for respectability.

When Mrs Davis came back from church she tried to describe the service but Charlotte shut her up, so she dropped the subject at once. She tried many others in the next two weeks, conscientiously anxious to earn her keep. Suppose Lady Brancaster was to get out her sketch-book and paints. Would she like to inspect the garden and think about ordering some new plants? Did she know how to play chess?

'You have brought down a fine selection of new novels, perhaps you would like me to read to you?'

'No, I should not!' exclaimed Charlotte, so vehemently that the poor woman jumped, and she felt a spark of compunction. 'I beg your pardon, it is just that I do not care for reading aloud.'

She could not bear the comparison with

happy evenings at Hartwood and Kit reading the *Waverley Novels* to her by the library fire.

The luckless Mrs Davis did achieve something without knowing it. To escape the companionship of her companion, Charlotte took to going for solitary walks. She had always been so active that her recent apathy was really affecting her health. The fresh air and exercise did her good.

She kept away from the village. It was a poor place anyway and the cottagers had a pinched and threadbare look, though they seemed to have all the necessities of life and many of them were employed in or around the Manor. She chose to jump down from the upper bank of the ha-ha at the end of the garden and take her rambles through the fields and woods, walking rather fast and always carrying with her the burden of her guilt and unhappiness. One autumn day she had come to the lip of a small valley she had not discovered before—what in these parts they called a combe. She sat down on the trunk of a fallen tree and surveyed the view.

In front of her lay a meadow of lush grass, stoutly fenced with some sleek cattle grazing. The hanging woods on the opposite hillside were turning from green to golden brown. It had been July when the nightmare started, August when she left London. Now it was

October.

Charlotte fingered the gold locket she wore round her neck. Unfastening the chain, she took it off and pressed open the case with her nail. Inside was a portrait of Kit. How well she knew the dark outline of that proud head, the brilliant grey gaze, the mouth that was just going to smile. Tears blurred her vision. What a fool I am, she thought angrily, to walk all this way in order to moon over his likeness as though I was a sentimental school-girl. She snapped the locket shut, laid it down on the scaly surface of the tree-trunk and again studied the rustic scene.

A definite footpath had brought her to this place, it continued through a grove of trees on her left and she wondered where it went. Leaving her seat, she moved forward a few paces for a better view. The meadow with the cows lay in a kind of flat saucer at the mouth of the combe, which grew suddenly deep and narrow. She could hear the sound of running water. She also heard a faint rustling close behind her and turned very quietly, hoping for a glimpse of some wild creature.

What she saw was a little ragged boy, crouched beside the fallen tree. A dirty hand slid out, something shiny flashed in the light, and he was up and away.

Charlotte gaped after him. Then she

realized what the bright flash had been—her gold locket with Kit's portrait.

'Come back, you little thief!' she shouted, beginning to run.

He had taken the path downhill through the trees, she caught sight of him with another child, a girl. She shouted again and they went faster. The way was rough and steep, and though Charlotte was a good runner the low branches of the trees kept thwacking in her face, while the children could pass underneath. They vanished round a twist of the path and her heart sank for she felt sure she would not catch them now. To lose the precious miniature was one more added grief she could hardly endure.

She turned the corner and the children were there, a few feet away from her. The little boy had fallen and was lying on his face, the girl was bending over him.

'Get up, Jemmy,' she was saying urgently. 'Get up, do.'

'Has he hurt himself?' asked Charlotte. 'Well, it serves him right, for he is a very naughty boy. Is he your brother?'

The girl nodded. She was clearly terrified, but she stood her ground.

Charlotte picked up her locket and put it on, gazing uncertainly at the small boy. There was no sign of any visible injuries and she wondered if he was having some sort of seizure, he was gasping for breath and his eyes were closed; he seemed to be unconscious. She now saw that he was also most dreadfully thin, a pathetic little scarecrow of brittle bones.

'Poor little fellow, let me make you more comfortable,' she said gently, kneeling down on the muddy path and supporting him in her arms. 'Has he ever done this before?'

'Ay,' said the little girl, who was almost as thin as her brother. She said something in the thick local dialect that Charlotte could not understand. Something about empty stomachs.

They were hungry—so hungry that the child had fainted from the exertion of running down the hill. But why? Surely no one living in the countryside need go short?

At this moment Jemmy came round and saw Charlotte's face above him. His eyes glazed with terror, he cried out to his sister:

'Becca! Don't let them hang me!'

'My dear child, there is nothing to be afraid of,' said Charlotte, horrified that someone should have frightened so young a child with threats of that kind. He was quite beside himself and sobbed out his pitiful entreaties for some time before she and Becca between them were able to convince him that he was not bound for the gallows.

Asked where they lived, Becca nodded towards the combe. She said something about the Bottom, and Charlotte realized that this must be Badger's Bottom, a place mentioned by her housekeeper Mrs Mason as being very much despised by their local servants who came from the more prosperous part of the village.

'I think we had better take Jemmy home, and I will carry him for I am sure he should not walk. Is your father down there?' enquired Charlotte, who thought that he was probably the maker of hideous threats.

'He's in Australey.'

'Good gracious, whatever made him—Oh!'

Now she knew the origin of Jemmy's fear. If a man was transported, he had almost certainly been convicted of a crime which might have carried the death sentence.

'He took one of Squire Bracey's pheasants,' added Becca.

The devil he did, thought Charlotte. I should like to meet Squire Bracey. Clasping Jemmy's frail and dirty body against her pretty green walking-dress, she followed Becca down the hill. She could feel his heart pounding like a little animal in a wire cage. She thought of the last child she had held in her arms, her own baby Will. And of the pacher who, like herself, would never see his son again.

Then they turned another corner and she saw the hamlet of Badger's Bottom.

Nine cottages huddled along the dark bed of the combe. They seemed to be actually growing out of the steep slope which provided their back wall. The sun would never penetrate that miserable little street, it was buried too deep; the stone fronts were blotched with fungus and the rotting layers of thatch sagged like old mattresses. There was no glass in the tiny windows and none of the cottages had a garden. The sodden pathway and the nearby stream were littered and choked with refuse.

Charlotte came to a halt, staring. She had never imagined anything so forlorn as this rural slum.

Bracing herself she followed Becca, and although there was no one about in the street she was aware of eyes watching her from the low doorways; suspicious, frightened eyes in sunken faces. Becca took her into the fourth hovel in the row.

Charlotte was used to the smell of cottages; she had been brought up to visit the old and ailing tenants at Clutton. The stench of filth, damp and sickness that met her here almost defeated her, but she swallowed back her nausea and glanced around. There was one dark room with streaming walls and an earth floor. The familiar box-bed, usually closed like a cupboard during the day, was open and jutting forward. Lying on it Charlotte made out in the dim shadows what she took at first for a litter of puppies. Then she saw that they were children, younger and weaker even than Jemmy, so feeble that they could only lie there half naked under the thin shawl.

'Oh, miss—what is it? What's happened to Jemmy?'

The mother was a stooping, careworn creature who had lived too long in a constant state of calamity; she looked terrified but too exhausted to do anything useful, or even to become hysterical.

'It's nothing serious,' said Charlotte, depositing the small boy on a vacant corner of the bed. 'He has been running and he is a little tired. Have you—is there anything we could give him?'

Jemmy's mother showed her a mixture she had been pounding with a rusty spoon. As far as Charlotte could judge, it consisted of some stale crusts of bread soaking in water. The woman put the bowl on the table and laid three wizened carrots beside it.

'There's naught else.'

'I'll bring you some food from my house.

Something for all the children.'

'Would you, miss? Oh, God bless you, miss,' said the poor woman, beginning to cry.

It's iniquitous, thought Charlotte, why is no one doing anything to help them? Their neighbours must be quite inhuman. Investigating the cottages on either side she found out the answer: the neighbours too were very near to starvation, thay had nothing to spare.

I shall have to do something about them all, she thought. She had noticed that there was a lane running off at an oblique angle from the far end of the combe. On asking one of the cottagers, she was told that this was the shortest way to Pristock. She set off at a brisk pace for the Manor.

It was a beautiful day, so welcome after the wet summer, and everything in nature was glowing with colour and life. The poverty and squalor in Badger's Bottom seemed even more dreadful by comparison. She did not understand how and why people should be starving in the midst of plenty, though she now remembered Kit telling her that there was a great deal of rural poverty. She had not believed him. Were these the conditions he was trying to improve in his struggle to bring down the price of bread? How frivolous and empty-headed she must have seemed to him, indifferent to suffering, caring only for her own pleasure. She hurried along the lane, pierced by an entirely new kind of guilt.

Some time later she burst in on Mrs Davis to announce that there were forty people starving, right here on their doorstep and she was going to feed them.

'Poor creatures, how very distressing,' said Lydia Davis when she heard the details. 'But Lady Brancaster, will you not sit down and rest for a little? You look so hot.'

'I've no time to rest.'

Charlotte pulled the bell-rope and ordered the carriage. Then she went to see what food there was in the house. The cook was affronted by the news that her delicious preserves and pastries were going to be wasted on common labourers, but Charlotte paid no attention and Mrs Mason, the former housekeeper at Clutton, was eager to encourage any scheme that could banish the look of dumb, bewildered misery from the eyes of her young mistress.

Charlotte sat in the carriage surrounded by sacks of potatoes and turnips, a large cheese, freshly baked bread, eggs and butter, two pails of milk, a smoked ham, fruit, honey and some mutton pies that had been meant for her dinner. Mrs Davis insisted on accompanying her, and Charlotte could only hope she would not swoon at the sight and smell of

Badger's Bottom.

They drove as far as they could along the lane, until the going got too bad. Then they continued on foot, Charlotte and Mrs Davis with a basket in each hand, and Timms the coachman carrying a hamper. When they reached the combe most of the inhabitants had come out and were facing towards the lane with expressions of dazed disbelief. Charlotte thought they had been waiting there since she went away.

She heard them whispering to each other. 'Er's come back . . . Never reckoned er'd come back.'

Charlotte addressed the assembly.

'I am Lady Brancaster and this is Mrs Davis who lives with me at the Manor. We have brought some food for every family, and if you will go into your cottages we will visit you all in turn.'

No one moved, they just stood staring at the hamper and the baskets. Charlotte felt slightly apprehensive. They were half-crazed with hunger, suppose they started to fight over the food? She thought quickly and said to Lydia Davis in a low voice. 'If we were to give each person an apple and a piece of cheese, they would have something in their hands to be going on with.'

This worked very well. The hunger which

had made these people desperate had also dulled their natural vigour and independence, and once nibbling and munching a first sample of the feast in store they were perfectly easy to manage.

Charlotte and Mrs Davis spent over two hours dividing up the supplies, noting what else was particularly needed and learning the name of each family. Charlotte was curious to know why they were in such a wretched state. Surely things had not always been so bad?

Everyone had the answer: it was all on the account of the enclosures. In old times, back when Granny Tobin was a girl, the land around here had been common. Every cottager had been able to dig his vegetables, keep goats or a pig, even a cow. With that, and the money they could earn as day-labourers, folk had lived well. Granny Tobin, a tough and resilient old woman, remembered being sent to mind the geese, over yonder where Farmer Bell had his cattle. When the enclosures came the poor people lost their grazing rights. They hadn't space enough for a broody hen or a hive of bees.

They had been forced to rely on what they could earn as labourers. They had plenty of work during the war, only their wages had not kept pace with the rising prices, and this year they could no longer get work. Farmer

Bell wouldn't take them on, they didn't rightly know why.

'I hope you get parish relief?'

It was all they did get; it was just enough to prevent anyone from actually dying of starvation and having to be buried at public expense.

'Is there no help from your more fortunate neighbours? From the church? Does the Vicar visit you?'

'Parson don't come down the Bottom.'

'And your landlord? I suppose he doesn't come either?'

They shook their heads.

Which was what you might expect. Heartless and irresponsible, she wondered who he was. Perhaps the Squire Bracey who had behaved so inhumanly over the poached pheasant.

'Who is your landlord?'

The cottagers shuffled their ill-shod feet and displayed something like social embarrassment. Granny Tobin answered for them with the informality of great age.

''Tis your good man, my dear. Marquess o' Brancaster.'

CHAPTER SIXTEEN

'I simply do not understand it!' declared Charlotte for about the tenth time since returning to the Manor. 'Brancaster is the best, the most generous of landlords! It is unthinkable that he should allow any of his tenants to live in such dreadful conditions.'

Mrs Davis looked at her rather oddly when she paid this tribute to her estranged husband but merely remarked, as she had done several times already, that doubtless his lordship had never heard of Badger's Bottom.

'Yes, but why hasn't he? Why hasn't that Waller person kept him informed? And now I think of it, why has Waller not been near me since I arrived?'

Because the Pristock estate was relatively small and had been let to a reliable tenant, it had never been found necessary to employ a full-time agent or steward, and Kit's interests had been looked after by a Mr Waller, an attorney in the nearby town of Rimborne, who was supposed to make and carry out small decisions himself, while reporting anything important to Mr Ferris in London. Mr Waller had also to collect the rents, which were paid ultimately into Child's Bank. Mr

Ferris had explained most of this to Charlotte at the time of the separation, when she had been too miserable to pay proper attention.

'The Vicar too,' she continued. 'Those people are his parishioners. Why has he done nothing for them?'

'I am afraid Mr Abinger is an ineffective sort of man.'

'He must have some effect on his congregation.'

'That's the trouble, Lady Brancaster. Hardly anyone goes to church.'

She did not add, as you would know if you went yourself, there was not even a hint in her manner, and this must be counted in her favour. Lydia Davis had not been disgusted or frightened by the people in Badger's Bottom, and Charlotte had now begun to see her as a useful ally.

They agreed that the Vicar should be consulted, and next morning Charlotte paid an early call at the Parsonage. She was alone, having left Mrs Davis at home hunting for spare blankets. Kept standing on the doorstep by an inexperienced maid, Charlotte stepped into the hall in time to hear a high-pitched protest through a half-open door.

'No, Samuel. I won't have Lady Brancaster shown in here, and you ought not to ask it of me!'

So the parson's wife is too holy to meet an adulteress, thought Charlotte. Only yesterday such a rejection would have sent her cowering back into her shell, ashamed and humiliated. Today acting on behalf of those in far greater distress, she could ignore pious disapproval.

Marching towards the indignant voice, she flung open the door.

'I am very anxious to see you, Mr Abinger—Oh! I beg your pardon.'

It was not at all like Badger's Bottom, of course. The room was light and dry, with smooth boards instead of an earth floor, but the boards were unswept, the carpet bald and shabby, the yellow wallpaper faded to a dirty cream. A sulky fire in the grate was perhaps the only one alight on a crisp autumn morning, for the life of the family seemed to be crowded into this poorly furinished room. Unwashed breakfast dishes were still piled at one end of the table books and papers at the other. Several children were learning their letters in the space between. The Vicar had taken off his jacket and was standing in his shirtsleeves, while a woman in a cotton wrapper was mending a split in the waistband of what she would probably call his unmentionables.

'I'm sorry,' faltered Charlotte. 'I did not

realize . . .'

Mrs Abinger, scarlet with mortification, fled from the room without a word.

'Oh dear,' said the Vicar. 'Your ladyship has taken us unawares. I am afraid this is not quite the setting in which to receive—I reminded my wife that pride is unbecoming in people of our station, but females feel these things differently—if your ladyship will be pleased to take a chair.'

Charlotte sat down, while Mr Abinger got rid of his children and put on his coat. (Did he realize there was still a needle dangling from a thread and ready to stab him in in the back?) She was sorry that her own particular form of pride and touchiness had brought her bursting into a room where poor Mrs Abinger did not wish to invite a titled parishioner, and she literally did not know where to look, every object seemed to indicate straightened means and bad management.

It was easiest to begin at once on the subject of Badger's Bottom. The Vicar was a small, worried man; he clucked sympathetically and said the afflictions of the country people were dreadful to witness.

'Have you been to visit them lately?' She knew he had not.

'I fear I have been somewhat remiss. It's a long walk, I don't keep a horse—' He caught her eye, and his tone changed. 'The fact is, ma'am, I cannot bear to go there when there is nothing I can do. They don't understand: how should they? My predecessor did a great deal; the stipened was perfectly adequate twenty years ago. Nowadays I have a struggle to support my wife and family on the same income, and since Bell at the farm has refused to pay his tithes I can't conceal from your ladyship that we ourselves are on the verge of want.'

'Why won't Mr Bell pay his tithes?'

'He insists that he is ruined. I don't believe it myself, these farmers made a fortune during the war, you would think they must have saved for a rainy day. But there it is. The Bells have stopped coming to church, and if he will not attempt to succour those unhappy labourers, nothing I say is likely to influence him. Perhaps your ladyship may be more successful.

'I hope so,' said Charlotte.

Her interview with Mr Bell was even shorter and less satisfactory.

She met him coming out of one of the huge, tiled barns that surrounded his weathered grey farmhouse. The place was neatly kept, and the farmer greeted her civilly enough, though she felt there was a latent hostility behind his respectful manner. He was a broad, burly man with an obstinate mouth.

When he heard why she had come, he laughed. 'Take on more labour? And how do you suggest I pay for it? After my crops have all rotted in the wet and there's no money to look for this side of Christmas? Well, you wouldn't know about such things, my lady.'

'You have some fine cattle ready for the drovers. They will fetch a good price at Smithfield, I dare say.'

He was slightly put out by this knowledgeable remark, but he said quickly that he had a good herdsman and dairy-maid who needed no extra help. 'And as for making a profit, the rent'll swallow that up. Rain or shine, the rent still has to be paid.'

He stared at her almost insolently, as though thinking that his hard-earned guineas had bought her warm pelisse, soft beaver bonnet and polished half-boots.

'Your rent has been reduced every year since the war,' she reminded him.

This made him stare harder. 'Whoever told you that, my lady?'

'All Lord Brancaster's tenants have had their rents lowered.'

'Well, it's the first I've heard of it. Ask Mr Waller if you don't believe me.'

'I shall certainly do so,' said Charlotte, preparing to retreat with dignity.

'And I mean to call on him immediately,' she announced having reported these conversations to Lydia Davis. 'Timms can bring round the carriage at once.'

'Then I must not keep you or the horses waiting,' said the companion, getting up from the writing-table, where she had been poring over some lists.

'There is not the smallest need for you to come. I can see how busy you are here. When you have seen what we can spare we must order whatever else is needed from a warehouse.'

'Yes, of course. But if you are driving into the town, I think I should come with you. You ought not to go about unattended; I know that is one of the reasons Lady Rivers engaged me.'

'My mother is afraid of my getting into another scandal,' retorted Chrlotte. 'But there is nothing for you to worry about. I can promise I shan't elope with Mr Waller.'

Such levity threw Mrs Davis into a state of blushing confusion and Charlotte was able to escape before she had recovered.

Rimborne was a rustic market town built round a cobbled square with a noble cross in the centre. The grey walls everywhere and the complete absence of brick made the place seem rather drab. However there were some good stone houses, and Mr Waller the lawyer lived and carried on his profession in one of the best. Charlotte's arrival caused a mild panic among the clerks, which did not surprise her, for she had decided there was something fishy about this unjust steward who had neglected his master's tenants and failed to carry out his orders. As she waited in a small lobby she half expected he might try to avoid an interview and was preparing to use her rank as a weapon and to make a scene if necessary, when a loud voice from the next room declared, 'To be sure I'll see her. Show her in!'

The clerk, with an apologetic manner, ushered her into a warm, well-furnished office. No signs of poverty here.

'The Marchioness of Brancaster, sir.'

'My dear ma'am—deeply honoured—happy to make your ladyship's acquaintance at last.' Mr Waller rose to execute a deferential bow and sat down again rather hurriedly. 'Pray be seated, ma'am. And you can get out, Dempson. Shan't want you.'

Charlotte's first impression of Mr Waller was that he might have been living in Badger's Bottom himself, he was so extremely emaciated. And his skin was a ghastly waxen colour. His surroundings breathed prosperity. A large fire crackled in the grate and there was a scent of wood smoke, aromatic snuff, leather law-books—and something else, what was it?

'I have called on you, Mr Waller,' she began, 'because I have been looking into things in Pristock and I am not at all happy about the situation of some of the tenants there.'

'The tenants in Pristock?' repeated Mr Waller, leaning towards her with an air of vacuous solemnity.

Charlotte was enlightened. She had identified the smell of brandy.

'Better consult the estate map,' said Mr Waller.

He heaved himself upright, fumbling for his keys, and then collapsed across his desk with a loud groan, sweeping off a heap of documents, a heavy deed-box and the decanter that had been coyly tucked behind the deed-box. At the same instant the door flew open and a fair-haired young man rushed into the room.

'Papa, I am sure you are not fit to—Oh, my God! You must excuse my father, Lady Brancaster. He is ill.'

'Your father is drunk,' said Charlotte.

She left the house with her nose in the air.

So that accounted for everything that was

wrong at Pristock. She felt furiously angry, with the wretched Waller, with Mr Ferris in London, and with Kit, who had failed so dismally to practise what he preached. She would like to tell him what she thought of him as a model landlord . . . Only she could not do that, because he would not meet her or read her letters. In any case, he could claim that he was doing his best to improve matters, even if he sometimes made mistakes, while she had never thought seriously about helping the poor until yesterday. She was in no position to throw stones.

Her carriage, with the coronet on the door, was standing outside the lawyer's house, and she was aware of being avidly gaped at by every citizen of Rimborne who happened to be in the square. It was the first time since the scandal that she had been recognized in a public place and she did not enjoy the sensation. As she came down the steps a lady and gentleman were approaching on the pavement, and she paused politely to let them pass. The big red-faced man ignored the civility and said something to his wife, who dutifully averted her gaze.

Provincials, thought Charlotte, dating and pricing the lady's ugly bonnet. They don't even know how to administer a graceful cut.

She was about to get into her carriage when

the lawyer's son came running after her.

'Lady Brancaster, may I speak to you? There is something I want to explain—'

'I don't see what needs explaining,' she said coldly.

'It is very important, to my mother and my family at least. And I won't keep you long.'

She glanced at him. He was a good-looking boy of about her own age, with fair, wavy hair and very blue eyes. He had one great advantage: he was apparently the only person in Rimborne who did not wish to goggle at the notorious Lady Brancaster as though she was a freak at a fair. He had troubles of his own.

'I am in a hurry to get home,' she said, 'but if you care to ride with me part of the way, we can talk as we go.'

'That is kind of you, ma'am.' Seated beside her in the elegant chaise he began at once. 'You were right when you said my father was drunk. Perhaps you will be more inclined to pity him when you know the reason. He has a disease that may—that must—prove fatal. Well, there is no point in mincing words, he has a tumour. He is in more or less continual pain, so that brandy and laudanum provide his only relief.'

Charlotte was disconcerted. She wondered if he could be lying, but rejected the idea immediately.

'How dreadful for you all,' she said. 'I am sorry if I jumped to an unkind conclusion just now. Surely your father ought not to be working if his complaint is so far advanced?'

'I know he should not, only he is determined to keep on as long as possible. With six children to plan for—I am the eldest and my name is Dick, by the way—I am just down from Oxford and hoping to take orders. My younger brothers are still at school. We shall have to find ways of earning our living, and I suppose my sisters will have to go for governesses when they are old enough. You see, my father's income from his practice has almost ceased since he became ill. That is why he has behaved so badly over the Pristock estate.'

'I don't understand.'

Dick Waller fiddled with the blind cord. They were now jogging down the turnpike road.

'My father receives a very handsome retainer for acting as Lord Brancaster's agent at Pristock. During the last two or three years I am afraid he has been taking that money on false pretences. Nothing has been done, no repairs, the tenants' problems have been ignored. He has kept the account straight and that is all. When your ladyship came down here to live, he grew very nervous, and it was only then my mother and I realized how badly things had been neglected. We have not known what to do.'

'But why did you father think it necessary to conceal his illness? Surely he could not suppose that he would be turned off and abandoned in a time of such misfortune? He must have a very strange notion of Lord Brancaster! You seem to think him perfectly heartless, which I assure you he is not!'

'We have none of us met Lord Brancaster. He has never been down to Pristock. And however generous he might have been at the outset, he is bound to be angry when he discovers that my father has been virtually cheating him for the past three years. I was wondering—if it is not too much to ask— whether you would appeal to his lordship on my father's behalf?'

She had been caught in the trap of her own generous feelings. It was not easy to retreat.

'I suppose you know why I have come down here to live,' she said at last. 'Everyone in Rimborne must know! You saw the charming way those people behaved just now. So perhaps you can appreciate that I should not be the very best mediator to put your father's case to Lord Brancaster.'

He was contrite. 'How clumsy I have been,

I never considered—please forgive me. And as for the Braceys, I hope you will not let their bad manners disturb you. They are a couple of sanctimonious bumpkins.'

'Oh, was that Mr Bracey? He is the man who sent Jemmy Allen's father to Botany Bay.'

'Who is Jemmy Allen?'

She told him, and this led to the whole story of Badger's Bottom. By the time she had done, they had reached the Pristock turning, Timms had stopped the carriage so that they could go on talking, and Dick Waller was gazing at her in admiring astonishment.

'You have certainly taken on one of the labours of Hercules. Our distresses are nothing in comparison to the sufferings of those poor creatures. I should not have troubled you with them.'

She did not agree. She was discovering a new and unsuspected world. The plight of the destitute was something she had always known in theory (though not expecting to meet it in the quiet countryside a mile from her own door). The hardships and anxieties of people like the Abingers and Wallers she had never imagined. She had entertained plenty of the lesser gentry and minor clergy on the public reception days at Hartwood;

how many of them, she wondered, had been hiding some secret fear of calamity behind their bright, company faces? Her crusading zeal now included the Wallers, but what could she do for them? She felt certain that Kit would care for the cottagers in Badger's Bottom if necessary; she was not at all sure how he would treat Mr Waller, who had been negligent to the point of dishonesty. She knew from bitter experience how inflexibly hard Kit could be towards anyone who deceived and cheated him.

Then a completely new thought came into her mind.

'Why, what a fool I am! We need not inform Lord Brancaster after all. He made over the Pristock estate to me when we—he settled everything so that I should be independent. Your father can go on drawing his salary for as long as he is able and I will run the place myself, with your help. What do you say to that?'

'You are altogether too quixotic—'

'No, I'm not. I shall make you work very hard. We must reduce Farmer Bell's rent; he is a disagreeable person but he has been unjustly treated, and I dare say he will then be able to pay Mr Abinger's tithes and employ more day-labourers. In fact I shall make it a condition. And then I shall return

197

some of the enclosed land—'

'I am not sure that you will be able to do that. It is all leased to the farm and I doubt if Bell will agree to let it go, even if you use the rent as a bait for bargaining with.'

'That's a snag. The cottagers need their grazing rights, and space to plant things, more than they need wages.' She brooded for a moment. 'Haven't I any land that isn't leased to Farmer Bell?'

'You have the coverts, I think. My father told me once that Mr Townley, the late tenant, was a keen sportsman in his younger days and wanted the woods for preserving game.'

'That's the answer, then. We'll cut down a wood.'

CHAPTER SEVENTEEN

Charlotte soon chose a wood to demolish. It was close to the combe, on reasonably flat ground, and she set the Badgers (as she privately called her protégés) to the task of felling the trees and clearing the undergrowth. She would pay them for working there, at any rate to start with, but the land and its produce would belong to the families in the hamlet.

She rode over to Skerret Wood every day to see how things were going on, and was trotting along the lane one bright morning when she saw a figure hastening towards her and recognized Peg Tobin, the young aunt of Becca and Jemmy Allen—nearly all the Badgers were called either Robin or Allen.

'Why, what's the matter, Peg?' asked Charlotte, as she reached the panting girl, who could do nothing but roll her eyes and gasp for breath.

'The wood—my lady—'

'What's happened? Has there been an accident?'

'Squire Bracey,' said Peg, making a great effort. 'Says he'll arrest the men for trespass. And he's got a gun, my lady.'

'Oh, has he?' said Charlotte grimly.

She touched the horse's flank with her heel and rode on much faster down the lane, his smooth canter quickening into a gallop.

When the wood came into view she saw a scene like some dramatic incident in a painting; in the clearing, among the amputated tree-stumps with their fresh, pale wounds, the labourers from Badger's Bottom had been driven into a corner by two men armed with shot-guns—Mr Bracey and his gamekeeper. A little way off huddled the group of boys and girls who had come along to help clear the ground, some of the younger children crying pitifully. The wood was enclosed and the gate was round on the far side; Charlotte put her horse at the post and rails and she sailed neatly over and landed almost on top of Mr Bracey, who swung round in a flurry, waving his gun in her face.

'Put that thing down,' said Charlotte. 'If you don't know how to handle firearms, you ought not to be let loose with one!'

She heard one of the men guffaw.

Mr Bracey lowered his gun rather hastily. It was a handsome double-barrelled breech-loader and she had heard he was a notable sportsman.

'I beg your pardon, ma'am,' he said stiffly. 'You took me by surprise. I think you would be wise to retire. These fellows are in an ugly mood, as you can see, but I shall bring them to account, never fear. They shall be made to pay for their criminal acts!'

'What criminal acts?'

'They have been cutting down the trees,' he said in a voice of exasperation at her stupidity.

'Yes, I know. I told them to.'

'You *told* them— you have no right to do such a thing!' He exclaimed rudely. 'I have been shooting over this land for the past seven year. Townley invited me to do so when he grew too infirm.'

'Mr Townley is dead,' she reminded him, 'and I am giving this piece of ground for the village people to cultivate.'

'But Skerret Wood is the best covert in the country,' he protested, staring at her resentfully with his small angry eyes. He was the kind of man who would naturally value game, which he was allowed to kill, higher than human beings whom he could only bully. He repeated something about Townley giving him the shooting rights, and she felt a slight qualm, wondering if he had any legal tenure. It was just the sort of thing Mr Waller would have forgotten to tell anyone.

'Have you a lease?' she asked.

'It was a gentleman's agreement,' he said

201

grumpily.

'What a pity Mr Townley was too gentle-manly to think of mentioning it to Lord Brancaster's agents,' said Charlotte. 'I am sorry for your disappointment, but as we have nothing further to discuss—'

'One moment, ma'am! I've not finished here! If you wish to ruin your husband's property I suppose I cannot stop you. Indeed I suppose it is the kind of wanton malice one might expect, according to what we have heard. But those idle rascals over there have to be taught a lesson. That man with the spade made a vicious attack on me just now, and I mean to take him into custody and charge him with assault. I am a magistrate and it is my duty to see that the law is upheld.'

'In that case,' said Charlotte, who was now trembling with rage, 'may I point out that you yourself are breaking the law. You are trespassing on my land.'

He goggled at her, speechless, as this strange idea sank in. He must be very stupid, or he would not have treated her with insolence while assuming he could still shoot the Pristock coverts.

'You came here unasked and tried to interfere with my servants when they were carrying out my orders—'

'You can't call them servants,' he jeered. 'That scum!'

'I'm paying them,' she retorted. 'That's good enough in law, and if they threatened you, they did so while protecting my property. You put yourself in the wrong. I am now asking you, in front of witnesses, to leave quietly and take your henchman with you. If you make any more trouble, I shall complain to your brother-magistrates, if necessary to the Lord Chancellor.'

As Bracey and his keeper withdrew in high dudgeon, one of the men threw his cap in the air and shouted, 'Three cheers for her ladyship.'

The tree-cutters cheered, the children came running forward to jump and squeal round her long-suffering horse, and her small friend Jemmy caught at her stirrup—a much plumper, livelier Jemmy than the poor little basket of bones she had carried down into the combe, the day he made off with Kit's picture.

Mr Bracey went into Rimborne and demanded to see Mr Waller but was received by Dick.

'I assured him I had your authority,' he informed Charlotte, 'which put his back up, I can tell you. And do you know what he was trying to find out? Whether you had the right to make alterations at Pristock without the Marquess's permission! I told him to mind his own business—in a properly pompous, lawyer-like way, of course.'

Dick was proving a useful lieutenant and Lydia Davis was another. Charlotte was like a young general planning her campaign for the improvement of life in Badger's Bottom.

Of course there were setbacks. Some of the Badgers spent their unaccustomed riches on drink and then there were fights. The clean blankets she gave them soon became dirty in those insanitary hovels—one really should provide them with somewhere else to live. And when the women were given stuff to make clothes, it turned out that many of them hardly knew how to sew. During the hopeless days of near-starvation, mothers had lost the habit of passing on skills to their daughters.

'The girls should be going into service,' said Charlotte, 'but I'm afraid they are too uncouth at present. I should dearly love to have some of them here, only Mason has warned me that all our own maids will leave in a body if I do. Stuck-up little madams, I have a very good notion to try.'

'Take care, Charlotte,' said Lydia. She had been instructed to use her employer's Christian name, though she still found it rather difficult. 'If you turn off the maids, they will soon be starving too and you will have to think of a scheme for rescuing them.'

Charlotte laughed and said, 'I tell you what: we ought to start a sort of school to teach cooking and knitting and so forth. I wonder how one would set about it.'

'I believe Miss Hannah More has written some books about her work among the poor lead-miners on the Mendips.'

'Perhaps my sister Amelia would get them for us. She is the only person who ever writes to me in a sensible way.'

Charlotte had not expected to hear from Amelia, who was timid and pious and rather prim. She had been touched by the affectionate letters, full of small doings, descriptions of nature and animals, discussions of what she had been reading. Amelia said little about her private hopes, probably from a sensitive awareness that Charlotte herself had so little to hope for, but she sometimes mentioned her friend Mr Fulton or implied that if and when she married, Charlotte would be invited to visit her. Mary had never written and Lord Rivers only once. Charlotte thought he found the situation too painful.

'Your mother writes every week,' said Lydia.

They were sitting by the drawing-room fire

and she had just made the tea.

'Poor Mama! It is such a penance to her, she never knows what to say. She does not care to mention any of the people or parties or visits that I am cut off from, and as she has hardly any other topics, unlike Amelia, it is very difficult for her to fill her letters. Church on Sunday and then if she is lucky a headache on Tuesday or some rain on Friday—that is about all I am likely to hear from Mama.'

Lydia, looking hunted, asked if she would like some more tea.

'Thank you. Yes, I should.' Charlotte handed her the cup and saucer but refused to be diverted. 'Shall I tell you why I get on so well with my Badgers? It is because we do not embarrass each other, we do not despise each other. When one comes to measure degrees of suffering, of course there is no possible comparison. Besides which they are innocent victims. I am not innocent. It is simply that we are all outcasts from respectable society and that is a great bond.'

'Dear Charlotte, you must not entertain such horrible ideas. I hope you don't think I have ever despised or criticized!' Lydia squinted madly into the depths of her teacup.

Charlotte took pity on her.

'I beg your pardon, I should not have teased you with such nonsense. It was pretentious and affected.'

'I have never been subjected to any strong temptation.' Lydia was saying. 'I am not qualified to judge others. And a great love—the wild impulses of the heart—these are not easily overcome by a cold sense of duty.'

Charlotte could not make head or tail of this, until she realized that Lydia had been misled into thinking her a victim too: a woman who had been genuinely in love with her seducer and who was paying heavily for having married the wrong man.

It was impossible to admit the truth. She thought about Lydia, about Mrs Abinger at the Parsonage, Mrs Bell at the farm, Mrs Waller and her dying husband and her large family: she had met them all by this time and taken a close look at the lives which they accepted without bitterness or false heroics. What would such women think of her if they knew the real facts?

'You are less unhappy now, are you not?' ventured Lydia. 'Since you interested yourself in the Badgers?'

'Oh, yes,' Charlotte said quickly. 'I am lucky to have the means of doing something so useful.'

Her great reserves of mental and physical energy were being tapped, and there were hours on end when she was too absorbed in other people to be aware of her own personal tragedy or to miss Kit and Will. At night she was often so tired that she fell asleep at once.

Deep sleep had only one disadvantage. When she swam up to consciousness in the morning the immediate past had been blotted out, so that she imagined herself at Hartwood, and reached out instinctively towards Kit who ought to be beside her. The return to bleak reality was such agony that she could hardly summon up the courage to face another day.

CHAPTER EIGHTEEN

'Do you know, Lady Brancaster, that there is a man watching this house?'

Dick Waller came into Charlotte's drawing-room on a grey November afternoon. It was barely three o'clock but so misty that the lamps had been lit, for she was hard at work cutting out flannel for the Badger girls to make into petticoats when they attended her improvised school in the disused billiard-room.

'Watching the house?' she repeated. 'Good gracious, what kind of a man?'

'A big fellow, could be a prize-fighter only he's too genteel. He's been asking some very odd questions all over the village, and now he's hanging about outside your gate. I thought you might have seen him.'

'I haven't been out today. Mrs Davis has a feverish sore throat, so I thought I would remain within reach. But tell me more! What do you suppose this person wants?'

'Well, I have a faint suspicion: I think he may be one of those agitators who are going around the country stirring up the poor labourers to make trouble. You know, the sort of thing the Government was trying to suppress when they suspended Habeas Corpus.'

'Why should he come here? He cannot suppose that I am at all likely to lead a march on Westminster.'

'He might if he consulted friend Bracey,' said Dick with a grin. 'You have no idea what a reputation you have in the neighbourhood. You are regarded as a desperate Rad by some of our more fearful citizens.'

She was amused and wished that her brother-in-law Oswald could have heard this; he would have been impressed if nobody else was. Then she saw that Dick was growing serious.

'I think the Battle of Skerret Wood may have been misinterpreteted by some. I have actually been told that you never gave permission for the trees to be felled, that the unemployed labourers took the law into their own hands and that you then protected them out of a mistaken compassion. Of course I said this was nonsense, but if the story has spread as far as Taunton or even Bristol, it may have raised false hopes among the extreme Radicals.'

'You mean, they may have sent someone here to lead those poor men into mischief?' she said, aghast. 'That would be really devilish. They know nothing of politics and the law, some of them cannot read.'

'I know. I think I should like a word with this mysterious stranger. I had the impression he nearly spoke to me when I turned in here just now, but he changed his mind. I was on horseback then and he is is on foot. It would not have been easy to hold a private conversation.'

'Have you put your mare in the stables?'

'Yes. If you don't object, Lady Brancaster, I think I'll leave her there and just saunter down to the gate to see what our gentleman is after.'

'Yes, do. And then come back and tell me.'

When Dick had gone, Charlotte felt excited and disturbed. Puzzled too, for she could not quite believe in his Radical agitator. Although he did not share their views, Kit had always insisted that most Radicals were serious, law-abiding people, so she had never seen them as bogeymen.

She went upstairs and looked out of her bedroom window. She could see Dick walking down the drive; it was no great distance and the manor house was not grand enough to possess a lodge. The iron gates were closed. She could not see the mysterious watcher, which was hardly surprising, for he must either be standing behind her stone wall or among the dark hollies and evergreens on

211

the opposite side of the lane. She glanced a little to the left and then something unexpected caught her eye. It was a carriage, perhaps a gig or phaeton, tucked away out of sight on the verge of the lane. It would not be visible from the drive, nor from the front gate, being masked by a projection of the estate wall. And Dick had approached the house from the other direction. She could see it only because she was looking down from above. But who could the carriage belong to? Surely it must have some connection with the watcher at the gate? Straining her eyes, she went on peering down. The mist was patchy, it swirled slowly in currents, like water sliding over broken ground, and although the day was dull it was not yet dark. For a few seconds she caught sight of a liveried servant dressed in a violent plum colour which she had seen Mr Bracey's men wearing in Rimborne. This was extraordinary; Mr Bracey was the last person she could imagine conspiring with a political agitator. And then she was struck by a more sinister possibility.

It was generally believed that a great deal of the unrest in the country was being inflamed, not by Radicals, but by spies in Government pay, *agents provocateurs* employed by the Home Secretary Lord Sidmouth to hunt out sedition; luring potential rebels into some rash act or statement and then arresting them. That was something Mr Bracey would probably approve of. Dick had gone to find out the stranger's business and might make some provocative remark; suppose the whole thing was a trap? Charlotte ran downstairs, snatched up a shawl as she passed through the hall and out of the front door. She raced down the drive, dragging the shawl round her head and shoulders as she went. The cold air caught her breath in sharp stabs.

Pulling open the gate, she heard Dick saying, 'I agree. The English labourer is often worse off than a Negro slave.'

She saw his companion merely as a shadow against a background of shadows, but immediately to their left, among the evergreens, she saw someone move, so she called out a warning.

'Take care, Dick! Eavesdroppers!'

The man in the bushes was startled out of his hiding-place. Dick, turning around, saw him advancing and hit him. Four other men sprang into action and set upon Dick and his genteel prize-fighter—not one of their allies after all, for he landed the second assailant a crack on the jaw, just before Mr Bracey's gamekeeper jumped on him from behind and brought him down. Charlotte saw him clearly for the first time and screamed.

There was a great deal of noise and scuffling. Charlotte would have launched herself into the middle of it, only she was restrained by the village constable, who said quite kindly that this was no place for ladies.

'Let them go—let them go, you disgusting savages!' cried Charlotte.

'I'm damned if I do,' retorted Mr Bracey, who was now in command, having secured a not particularly glorious victory with five men against two. 'Disturbing the peace— that's enough to be going on with. I'll deal with them in the morning. They can spend the night in the lock-up.'

'That's ridiculous,' protested Dick. His mouth was bleeding and he was dabbing it with a handkerchief. 'I didn't mean to start a brawl, but when fellows creep up on one from behind, it is natural to defend oneself. I'll come and see you in the morning if you want me, sir, and I'm sure this gentleman will do the same.'

'He's a damned Jacobin. I heard some of the treasonable nonsense he was spouting just now.'

Everyone looked at the second prisoner, who was brushing the mud off his coat in a grim silence. He certainly looked murderous.

Charlotte found her tongue. 'He's not a

214

Jacobin. You can't lock him up, Mr Bracey.'

'And why not, pray? I'm not trespassing on your land this time,' sneered the magistrate. He became even more suspicious. 'Are you acquainted with the fellow?'

'Of course I am. That is my—that is Lord Brancaster.'

The gamekeeper and the constable both stepped back as though they had burnt their fingers. Another of the men let out a low whistle, while Dick said, 'Oh, my God!' seeming more alarmed than reassured.

Mr Bracey, slower-witted than the rest, said, 'I don't believe it.'

Kit addressed him in an icy voice. 'Whether you believe it or not, my good sir, is a matter of complete indifference to me. If you want to put me in the local round-house, you are welcome to try but I fancy you will have to do it single-handed. Thank you.'

This was to one of Bracey's servants who had rescued his hat, which had fallen in the road.

'I beg your pardon, my lord,' said Bracey stiffly. He must have decided that such deliberate rudeness was a proof of aristocracy, perhaps it was the only one he was capable of recognizing. 'I heard reports of a stranger in the village, questioning some of the disaffected classes, poachers and the like. It never

215

entered my head that this might be your lordship. I was entirely taken by surprise.'

'I can't imagine why. You encouraged me
to come here. I suppose you are the Mr
Bracey who wrote me a long letter full of facts
you felt I ought to know? I am most grateful
for your interest in my affairs, but I hope you
will keep out of them from now on.'

He turned his back on the magistrate and
said something to Dick.

Mr Bracey stood for a moment, and then
stumped off at the head of his troops. It
should have been a pleasure to Charlotte to
see him routed yet again, but she did not feel
triumphant. She was too badly shaken
herself. There had been a brief moment
during that strange scene when she had
wanted to save Kit from being hurt and man-
handled by those bullies. Now she had begun
to wonder why he was here. He had received
a letter from Mr Bracey; what sort of letter
could that hateful man have written to bring
him secretly to Pristock? She shivered and
pulled the shawl closer.

Kit glanced at her for the first time and
spoke with a distant formality. 'You are cold,
we had better go indoors. Will you not intro-
duce your friend?'

Dick was looking anxious. She said: 'This
is Mr Richard Waller.'

216

'Then you are one of the people I have come to meet.' Kit held out his hand but the words sounded ominous. 'Your father too, of course. Perhaps you will tell him.'

'I am afraid my father's health—I know there is a great deal that needs explaining,' stammered Dick. 'Lady Brancaster has been very kind.'

'I am sure she has,' said Kit smoothly.

He held open the gate for her to pass through.

She had a horrible premonition. She and Dick had been hand in glove since the day they met, combining in their efforts to thwart Mr Bracey and only too ready to let him know it. Had he taken a mean revenge by informing her husband that she was carrying on an intrigue with the son of his agent? It was the sort of thing a coarse-grained person like Bracey might actually believe. And Kit? Well, she knew what Kit thought of her by now.

They walked up the drive, Dick coming with them as he had to fetch his horse from her stables—which seemed to accentuate their intimacy. He was making everything worse, poor Dick, by being so obviously nervous. She knew this was on account of his father's failings and the fear that Kit might not be so lenient as she had been. Dick's admiration for her was romantic, respectful and altogether undemanding and she was sure he had never imagined that he might have compromised her; he was very innocent, it was probably something to do with wanting to be a clergyman. Yet to a jealous husband his manner must seem blatantly guilty.

Charlotte herself did not say a word.

When they reached the front door it was Kit who asked Dick, quite kindly, if he would come in and have his cut seen to.

'Thank you, my lord, but there's no need. The bleeding has stopped and I am expected at home.'

He made his escape.

CHAPTER NINETEEN

Charlotte walked into the warm house, into the drawing-room where she had been peacefully cutting out flannel petticoats half an hour before. They were strewn all over the furniture. Kit followed her in.

'Good God, Charlotte—what an untidy room!' he exclaimed, just as he might have done when they were living together.

He then seemed to feel that this was a breach of good manners, that he had abdicated his right to make husbandly remarks, for he coloured with embarrassment. Charlotte did not notice. She had just realized what she minded most about his lurking outside her gate; it was the idea that his distrust of her should have induced him to sink so low.

'Did you have to come and spy on me yourself?' she could not help asking.

'Is that what you think I was doing?'

'If Bracey told tales about me, I can guess what they were—'

'Then you are considerably better off than I am,' said Kit rather crisply, 'for he left me quite in the dark. His letter was the most unmitigated rubbish I ever read. Only two things were plain; you have cut down a valuable plantation and one of us is being swindled.'

'Oh,' said Charlotte, feeling a little foolish.

He crossed to the fireplace and stood looking down at the burning logs, so that she was able to study him closely which she had not dared do before. Out in the misty dusk nobody had seemed quite real. Here, alone with him in a lighted room she was affected as she had always been by his physical presence. She had forgotten how tall he was and the splendid breadth of his shoulders under the dusty coat. His jet black hair had been tousled by the scuffle in the lane and there was a bruise on one cheekbone. The eyes were veiled by those long, dark lashes, so surprising in that vehemently masculine face.

'I asked Ferris,' he continued, 'whether he knew why you should be cutting down trees. He didn't, but he told me you had started drawing money from the bank. I decided that you must be making some improvements and I felt a certain anxiety in case you were being cheated by some dishonest landscape-gardener.'

'Oh,' said Charlotte again.

'So I came to look for these improvements, and I must say I was astounded when I saw them.'

'But I haven't made any,' she said, her

220

mind running on follies, temples and the Inigo Jones colonnade at Hartwood which she had turned into a conservatory.

'Haven't you? I gather the lives of the people at Badger's Bottom have been improved out of all knowledge.'

'Have you been to Badger's Bottom?'

'Yes, and to Skerret Wood. It is amazing what you and young Waller have done in so short a time. Though I think in the long run it would be wise to pull down those dreadful hovels and build new houses in a better situation.'

'Do you?' she asked eagerly. 'So do I, only it is difficult to know where, with the land having been enclosed and then let. That has been the real disaster, you know: even worse than the lack of employment. One cannot blame the men who took to poaching. Jemmy's father was transported to Botany Bay. I expect you saw Jemmy and Becca . . .'

Relief had gone to her head like champagne, and there was so much to tell about Badger's Bottom. It seemed natural to be pouring out a jumble of facts and opinions to Kit. Suddenly she remembered, and checked herself, flushing. 'I'm talking too much.'

'There's something you still haven't said.'

'Is there?'

'You haven't said: "What is the point of

setting up as a champion of the poor, dividing your time between Westminster and Manchester, when you neglect your own estates and allow your tenants to starve?" It's a very pertinent question and no one has a better claim to ask it than you, Char. All things considered.'

He sounded deeply chagrined, and any lingering desire to score off him vanished immediately.

'I was very surprised at first,' she admitted. 'However, I soon understand why it was that you knew so little about conditions at Pristock.'

'You are generous,' he said, after she had explained. 'But I still don't understand why none of these people appealed to me, either directly or through Ferris. Not the cottagers, I mean Bell or the parson or the unfortunate Waller? Surely he cannot have thought I should persecute a sick man? What sort of an inhuman monster do they take me for?'

'They see you as a very rich lord a long way off and they are afraid of you, because you have power over so many lives.'

Including mine, she thought, in the uneasy pause that followed. She was summoning up the courage to ask about her little boy; if only she could do it without breaking down.

'How is Will?'

'Oh, he's doing splendidly,' said Kit in an unusually hearty manner. 'Talking a lot more. I've given him a puppy.'

'I'm so glad,' said Charlotte in a loud, clear voice.

There was another silence.

Then he said, 'I want to ask you a question, Charlotte. Please give me a truthful answer. I promise I won't be angry or unkind, no matter what you say.'

She waited, cold with apprehension.

'Are you still in love with Gerard?'

'Good heavens, no! I never was,' she said impulsively.

'Well, that's encouraging,' he managed a slight smile. 'Once one is convinced of that, the worst is over.'

'But I never loved him,' she repeated and realized what a shocking confession it was. Considering all the trouble and misery she had caused, a lifelong passion would have been more easily excused.

'You ran away with him.'

'No,' she said in a low voice, 'I ran away from you. No one had ever treated me so harshly before, so I was frightened and that made me feel ill-used—even though I deserved everything you said to me, I've realized that since. At the time I wanted to pay you out. So I got Gerard to escort me to the Rendals, only Sally would not have me, and we were obliged to put up at an inn—but you have heard all this from my father. Didn't you believe him?'

Kit hesitated. 'To tell you the truth, I don't think he believed himself. I imagined it was a story you and your mother had concocted in order to salvage my wounded pride. Your father begged me to take you back, but I couldn't do it. I couldn't trust myself to live in the same house with you while I thought you were pining for Gerard. I should have made you wretched and we should both have suffered torments.'

Charlotte asked, 'Would you have forgiven me if I hadn't gone off to Berkshire?'

'Of course. I wrote to you from London. The letter reached Hartwood the day after you left.'

They gazed at each other across an abyss of their own making.

'Oh, how wicked I have been!' Charlotte burst out in a rush of remorse. 'Wicked and selfish and stupid. My father said I was unfaithful to you because you would not take me to Scotland on the day I wanted to go, and I am afraid he was right. I am so sorry, Kit. And so ashamed.'

Tears choked her, she covered her eyes with her hands. Through the tumult of her own grief she heard him move so suddenly that he kicked the fender and the tongs clattered in the grate. He was beside her, plucking away her fingers so that he could see her face.

'Don't cry, love,' he murmured. 'It's all over now, like a bad dream.'

Charlotte gasped and clung to him as though she was drowning.

All the chairs in the room were draped with strips of flannel, so he picked her up and carried her back to the fireplace, where he knelt down cradling her in his arms. For about ten minutes she could do nothing but hold on to him and sob into his shoulder. At last he persuaded her to look up.

'You've been crying too,' she said huskily.

'Not for the first time.'

'What a hateful creature I am, to have hurt you so!'

'Do you want to make amends?' he asked, smiling. 'You must stop scolding yourself and kiss me properly.'

The kisses were rapturous, renewing lost pleasures that were incredibly sharp and sweet after four months of privation. As they nestled in the firelight she was filled with an exquisite release of joy. She had carried an interior rack of misery with her for so long; now the screws had been untwisted. While

Kit held her so close she was paradoxically as free as air.

They did not speak. The only sounds in the room came from the hissing logs and the heartbeats of the bracket clock softly counting away the time which for them stood still.

Until the door opened and an artificially bright voice began: 'Where are you, Charlotte? I thought I heard a gentleman arriving and I felt perhaps I should—*Oh dear!*'

Lydia stood staring at them in dismay. She had left her sickbed, conscious of her duty as a chaperone, and scrambled into her clothes; because she was feeling so ill she had put on her cap the wrong way round. The effect of this on top of her horrified expression, was so ludicrous that Charlotte could not utter a word, she was so busy struggling not to laugh.

Kit had more self-command. He got up at once.

'How do you, Mrs Davis? We have not met before. I am Charlotte's husband.'

'Her *husband*?' bleated Lydia. 'Thank goodness for that! I mean—I beg your pardon, my lord—so stupid of me, I thought—'

What she had thought was transparently obvious: abandoned Charlotte, reclining on the hearthrug, in the arms of a lover.

Charlotte had now pulled herself together.

'My dear Lydia, you should not have come down. I am sure you are still feverish.'

'A little perhaps. It doesn't signify. And I promised Lady Rivers I would never leave you alone to receive callers, though Lord Brancaster is hardly—'

'Hardly an ordinary caller, ma'am,' said Kit gravely.

Lydia said she was afraid there might not be anything suitable for his dinner.

'And I must tell them to get a room ready for his lordship and make sure they air the sheets—'

This time it was Kit who nearly disgraced himself.

Charlotte said, 'Do go back to bed, Lydia. Mason and I will see to everything.'

'What a very silly woman,' said Kit, when she was safely out of earshot. 'I think your mother might have chosen a better companion for you.'

'Poor Lydia, I won't hear a word against her. Generally she is very sensible. And she was right about the dinner—I will make sure there is enough for you to eat.'

Kit said he ought to send a message to his groom, who had been instructed to bring the curricle at five o'clock to the corner of the turnpike road. These arrangements did not take long, but it was long enough. Charlotte had time to think and her illusion of happiness was shattered. Sadly she occupied herself in folding up the pieces of flannel that were still festooned over the furniture.

'What were you doing with all that stuff?' enquired Kit.

'Cutting out petticoats for my sewing class.'

'I thought you might have been rending your garments.'

When she did not respond, he asked: 'What's wrong Char?'

She sat down on the sofa and began to rearrange the neat pile of cloth.

'It's too late,' she said tragically.

'For what?'

'You cannot live with me again after what has happened. I shall be cut by our old friends, no one will receive me, and if you take me back you will very likely be ostracized as well for condoning my adultery. And those who are not shocked will laugh at you and hold you in contempt. I could not endure that.'

'Plenty of people are laughing already,' he said coolly. 'No, not on your account, my darling, so don't look so stricken. My efforts to bring down the price of bread are thought highly amusing.'

It struck Charlotte for the first time that Kit might have lost his taste for Almack's and other fashionable haunts because he found himself politically alienated from men he had known all his life. This had never occurred to her before. How childish I was, she thought regretfully. She must not be childish now.

'Those who laugh at your theories still respect you as a man. They won't, if you insist on consorting with your disreputable wife. Suppose I returned home with you tomorrow—'

'Doors would be shut in your face and it would be very unpleasant. Yes, I know. And whether they were shut in mine is immaterial, for I should not dream of entering a house where you were not welcome.'

(Unlike Gerard, she noted gratefully.)

'There is one thing you probably don't understand,' Kit continued, coming to sit beside her on the sofa. 'Society is a severe judge, but there is just one crime that is always conveniently forgotten in time: a scandal caused by the differences of a husband and wife who are later reconciled. Time is the governing factor. If we were to go abroad for a year or two, we should return to find that there was nothing very disagreeable to overcome. A little awkwardness, that is all.

And that would soon pass.'

'Are you sure?' she asked, hardly daring to believe him.

'Certain. I've known it happen several times before. We are not the first couple to make a public exhibition of our private follies.'

'I can never follow all these distinctions. But then I must be very dense, for I never properly understood the rules of marriage— the unwritten rules, I mean—which is why I made such a terrible mistake. I see that now. Even though I still don't see why . . .' Her voice trailed off uncertainly.

'I dare say you feel it is unjust,' suggested Kit, 'that wives are condemned for sins which their husbands may commit with impunity. Remember that we don't all try to take advantage of that concession. I doubt if I shall ever be unfaithful to you.'

This startled her. It was something she had never contemplated. He was the most attractive man she had ever met; in spite of that, and his reputation before he married her, she had never expected him to look at another woman. How abominably conceited she had been.

'That's not what I was thinking of,' she said rather hurriedly.

But how to explain her real difficulty? She

could not say, 'I thought it would not matter if I had a lover'. She now recognized that this attitude of mind had in itself been a betrayal of love.

And it was no good citing her cousin Olivia as an example; Olivia's family had married her to Mr Chance, as dull as ditchwater, because he was so rich. To compare their marriages was an insult. In any case it was not the Chances or the Rendals who had misled and confused her in the first place.

She took a deep breath. 'There are some marriages of true affection where the wife is not always faithful.'

'You are speaking of your parents,' he said gently.

'I grew up knowing about Mama, and it did not seem very important, since my father did not mind—'

'What makes you so certain that he does not mind?'

She was taken aback. 'Do you imagine he did, to begin with? About Lord St Eudo?'

'By the time St Eudo came on the scene I dare say he was pretty well resigned.'

'Was there someone else before?'

'Two or three, I believe.'

She gazed at him, her eyes huge. 'Tell me.'

'I don't know the details. I was ten years old when your parents married; what I have heard comes chiefly from Olivia. They were thought to be very much in love; he certainly was, and I dare say she was too. Within a few years she had plunged into a wild infatuation for a man called Humphrey Dacre—you won't remember him, he was killed quite early in the war. Your father begged her to give up the affair, but she would not listen, and he could not bring himself either to compel her by force or to live apart from her. After Dacre's death she was heartbroken, until she fell in love with his successor. St Eudo has lasted longer than the others, nearly eight years.'

Charlotte was so much astonished by this account of her parents' marriage that at first she could do nothing but snatch at fragments of the newly disclosed truth. What unhappiness they must have concealed—Mama so selfish and weak, Papa so unselfish and weak. No wonder they had both been so frantic the day she went back to Berkeley Street and blamed her mother for her own reckless indiscretion. . . . Many ambiguous shades of meaning were now made plain.

She turned to Kit and said very seriously, 'I promise you I will never, never let myself be drawn into another entanglement not even a flirtation. It is too dangerous for someone like me. I take after Mama.'

'I don't think you do. Not now. Though I confess that was my first thought when I read Gerard's letter. I thought you had taken the first step down a well-worn road. That's why I was so hard on you, my poor little love: I was determined to stop you, at whatever cost to us both. So I behaved like a perfect brute. Only I miscalculated, and instead of being frightened into good behaviour you ran away. You are altogether a stronger character than your mother.'

'And you than my father. Poor Papa, I am so sorry for him. Though I dare say you have no great opinion of his merits as a husband.'

'On the contrary, I have a high regard for him. At least he knows his own limitations. Which is more than I can say for myself.'

'What does that mean?'

'What do you suppose I was doing, loitering outside your gate and getting myself mistaken for a Radical agitator? I was desperate to see you and I was trying to beat down my pride sufficiently to come in here and tell you so.'

Charlotte's household produced a passable dinner and a rather indifferent bottle of port for his lordship to drink afterwards. This started a new train of thought: he wondered if they should visit Portugal.

'I believe the landscape is interesting and

233

the climate excellent. It would be somewhere new for us both.'

The servants had been dismissed and they were alone at the dining-room table, for she had stayed with him after the covers were removed. They could not bear to be parted. She did not answer straight away. Kit chose a walnut from the dish in front of him, cracked it and gave her the open shell with the nut lying inside, shaped like a miniature skull.

'I don't think we ought to go and live abroad,' she said slowly.

'My dearest Charlotte,' he protested, preparing to be kind but firm, 'there is no need for you to go on punishing yourself through an exaggerated sense of guilt—'

'Oh, that's not the reason,' she said cheerfully. 'I should like to spend a few weeks on the Continent, it would be charming to have another honeymoon, only I don't think you should leave England for too long. You cannot wish to abandon your fight against the Corn Laws, and I shall certainly never complain or try to dissuade you, now that I understand how much these bad laws affect people. I find the Game Laws are very stupid—did you know that pheasants don't belong to anyone but only gentlemen are allowed to shoot them? Well, of course you must know, as you're a landowner. Where was I? Oh yes. I have schemes of my own: I want to go on helping the Badgers and others like them, those who live in destitute villages where there is an absentee landlord, or where no one is able and willing to do anything useful. I am sure I shall have plenty of scope. Do you think I could live with you very quietly in the country while the scandal dies down? Would that serve as well as going to Portugal?'

'Yes, I expect it would,' he said, looking at her with a rather dazed expression, a mixture of exasperation and delight. 'What an extraordinary girl you are, Char. And what a fool I've been, boring you to death with economics, when I could have won you over instantly, just by taking you to see one hungry village.'

'Yes,' she agreed. 'Why didn't you?'

Kit handed her another walnut. 'I wanted to protect you. I felt you ought to be shielded from sights that might prove too painful for your youth and sensibility . . . I *have* been a fool!'